Praise for *Al*

"Fast, punchy, and funny. Abelman combines a warm-hearted comic look at the terrors of creation with nuggets of history and context. It's one of those rare escapist reads where you come out a bit smarter than you went in."

—Eric Coble, playwright (*The Velocity of Autumn, Bright Ideas*)

"I literally couldn't stop smiling. *All the World's a Stage Fright* is a valentine and Abelman's unfailing love of Cleveland theater comes through loud and clear."

—Vicky Bussert, Director of Music Theatre, Baldwin Wallace University

"Funny. Utterly delightful. Totally believable. Bob Abelman takes his readers on an enchanting journey across the footlights and gives us a hilarious, but true-to-life, glimpse into the madcap and magical process of putting on a play. It is charming and informative, full of insight and introspection, and a story that brings smiles from the first page and a tear or two by the end. I enjoyed every moment of it."

—John Rubinstein, Tony Award-winning actor (*Pippin, Ragtime*)

"A rare, first-person peek into the mind of a theater critic with humor that pours from every page."

—Nathan Motta, Artistic Director, Dobama Theatre

"A clever, amusing exploration of the theatrical process."

—Misha Berson, former chief theater critic, *Seattle Times*

"An entertaining romp. This book is for you if you like theater and Shakespeare."

—Roe Green, Cleveland theater philanthropist

All the World's a Stage Fright

Misadventures of a Clandestine Critic

— A NOVELLA —

Bob Abelman

Published in partnership with
Cleveland Jewish News

Gray & Company, Publishers
Cleveland

Gray & Company, Publishers
www.grayco.com

ISBN 978-1-938441-97-4
Printed in the United States of America

Contents

Preface 7

3 left 26 near 0 pinch 9

Doing a Plimpton 12

I Fear Shakespeare 16

What Curse 19

Thespian Troupe 44118 23

Mount Everest 29

Run 31

The Chronicle 40

Damn Shakespeare 44

Critics Are Hated and So Excoriated 49

Casting Call 56

Climb Every Mountain 60

Ten Syllables, Five Stressed 61

Let the Healing Begin 65

Thin Skin 70

Meet-and-Greet 76

Write on Cue 81

Killing Off Adam 86

Playbill 90

Suppressing Shakespeare 91

A Sense of Foreboding 95

Some Quality Time 99

Lenny in the First Row 104

6 CONTENTS

Reflections of Opening Night 108

Come On and Kiss Me, Kate 114

The Reviews Are In 117

Moving Forward 121

The Road Not Taken 123

Acknowledgments 127

Preface

Have patience and endure.

Much Ado About Nothing (Act IV, Scene I)

*T*O NON-THEATER LOVERS," wrote actor Joel Grey in an opinion piece in *The New York Times* shortly after the worldwide outbreak of the coronavirus pandemic hit the U.S., "lamenting the closing of Broadway in the face of so much widespread suffering may seem, at best, frivolous. But for many of us, this tragedy has been made that much more devastating by having to face the nightmare without the laughter, tears, and sense of community that a night in the theater delivers."

The same thing happened in London between 1603 and 1613, when the Globe Theatre and other playhouses were shut down for a total of seventy-eight months—more than sixty percent of the time—because of recurring bubonic plague outbreaks. And there are some lessons to be learned.

From 1603 to 1604, when one in five Londoners succumbed to the disease, a quarantined William Shakespeare wrote *Measure for Measure*. And when the plague returned in the summer of 1606 and killed more than one-tenth of the city's population, Shakespeare was putting the finishing touches on *King Lear, Macbeth*, and *Antony and Cleopatra*.

In short, some of Shakespeare's best, most creative writing was done in the shadow of a pandemic. Imagine what awaits us when the coronavirus runs its course.

And though the plague is mentioned in *The Tempest*, *Timon of Athens*, *Romeo and Juliet, Richard III, Twelfth Night*, and *King Lear*, no one dies of the disease in Shakespeare's works. Not one person. So while his plays and sonnets were by no means a cure, they were certainly a source of most welcome respite from the suffering.

They still are. In immediate response to the coronavirus, London's National Theatre Live offered a free streaming of its production of the comedy *Twelfth Night* on YouTube and Shakespeare's Globe Theatre launched an online series called "Love in Isolation," where actors shared some of the greatest words ever written by Shakespeare from their places of quarantine. Actor Sir Patrick Stewart recited all of Shakespeare's sonnets, one each day, on his Instagram account. His first post boasted more than 464,000 views and 3,800 comments.

And I wrote this fictionalized memoir of a true lover of theater, which is also a love letter to Shakespeare. *All the World's a Stage Fright* is dedicated to those who have boldly and beautifully performed his words upon the stage and will do so again when this pandemic has passed. And it is written for those like me—like you, I think—who need Shakespeare's prose and poetry now more than ever.

CHAPTER 1

3 left 26 near 0 pinch

All the world's a stage, and all the
men and women merely players.

As You Like It (Act II, Scene VII)

*W*HENEVER I LOOK through the press releases sent to me
by the city's professional playhouses that announce
their roster of new season productions, the former actor in
me gets the itch to perform in one of them.

That feeling always fades, like a phantom ache where a
surgically removed limb used to be, when I remember that
the name Asher Kaufman pays the bills better when in the
byline of a show's review than in its playbill. But this time
the itch was agitated by Mark, the assistant managing editor
of the weekly Cleveland newspaper that hired me as its
theater critic.

"What if you wrote a series of articles about what takes
place on the other side of the proscenium arch while in an
actual production?" he suggested during one of our infre-
quent and always unproductive meetings about ways to
drive up the paper's readership. This one took place over
a light snack at Corky & Lenny's, where Mark decided

to forego the snack and have the Reuben and fries. "You know," he said loudly, in competition with the lunchtime din of the deli, "do a Plimpton."

George Plimpton was an American journalist who, in 1963, attended the preseason training camp of the Detroit Lions of the National Football League under the pretense of being a backup quarterback. It wasn't much of a pretense once he stood under center and called out signals with an aristocratic inflection from a different era. Also, the lanky, Harvard-educated Plimpton was not an athletic-looking man unless the sport was Division III badminton. He was thirty-six years old at the time, which was older than some coaches on the Lions' sideline. Nonetheless, he was granted permission to run five plays in an intrasquad scrimmage so he could write about the experience.

The first play was called "3 left 26 near 0 pinch" which, despite the convoluted nomenclature, was a basic running play. Upon taking the snap, Plimpton promptly bumped into his own offensive guard and fumbled the football for a five-yard loss.

The second play, "Green right 3 right 93," was a pass that ended prematurely when Plimpton took one step back after the ball was snapped and fell down on his own volition, succumbing to the pressure of the moment, gravity, and the demons in his head.

During the third play, Plimpton managed to take several steps back but was met by a 300-pound defensive lineman named Roger "Rhinofoot" Brown, who yanked the football right from the quarterback's soft, shaking, ink-stained fingers and lumbered to the end zone for an easy touchdown. And so on.

Yeah, "do a Plimpton" sounded like a grand idea.

But then Mark reminded me that Plimpton's embarrassing little excursion into participatory journalism resulted in a series of popular articles in *Sports Illustrated,* which was then turned into the bestselling book *Paper Lion* and, later, into a movie starring Alan Alda as Plimpton.

I had stopped listening by then because all I heard was "3 left 26 near o pinch" and the sound of stampeding rhinos. Now I can't stop wondering who would play me in the movie.

CHAPTER 2

Doing a Plimpton

By the pricking of my thumbs,
something wicked this way comes.

Macbeth (Act IV, Scene I)

I'VE BEEN WRITING theater reviews for over twenty years and have been with the *Cleveland Jewish Chronicle* for most of them, so it was certainly time to mix things up for me and my readership. Mark's suggestion that I be a clandestine critic—an embedded arts journalist—certainly had merit, and I agreed to look into this idea just as he was about to channel a motivational Knute Rockne in the locker room at halftime and humiliate us both in front of the Corky & Lenny's regulars. Mark is pasty and paunchy from rarely leaving his desk in the light of day, so playing him in my movie would be Jason Alexander from *Seinfeld*.

Playhouse Square is Cleveland's downtown theater district. It is one of the largest in the nation, second only to New York City, and includes meticulously renovated venues constructed in the early 1920s as houses for vaudeville and movies. One plays host to the Cleveland Play House, the oldest permanent professional regional theater in the United States and a Tony Award winner. Others offer top-

tier national Broadway tours and Cleveland's classic reper-
tory company, Great Lakes Theater. There's also a thriving
professional theater scene consisting of smaller stages on
the near east and west sides of the city that are producing
innovative, avant-garde, and contemporary plays as well as
original works by local playwrights.

Back at the office, I scanned the list of productions to be
performed by these theaters, matched them with my skill set
as a performer, and figured I would audition for the musical
Sweeney Todd: The Demon Barber of Fleet Street to be staged by
North Coast Theater.

Several years ago, the company formerly known as
North Coast Shakespeare Ensemble moved from an archaic
venue on the east side of the city to the downtown Hedley
Theatre, expanded its offerings from all things Shakespeare,
and renamed itself accordingly. Its season now includes a
musical and two modern plays to go with two Shakespeare
productions in an effort to attract a larger pool of potential
subscribers and challenge the company's core of classically
trained performers.

I am not a fan of Shakespeare. I'm certainly familiar with
the work and my occupation requires that I review productions of it whenever and wherever they're staged, but I'm
never looking forward to reviewing them and I've never performed Shakespeare when I was seeking work as a professional actor. Just not in my wheelhouse.

I tended to do musicals during my performing years,
perhaps because Shakespeare never wrote one. It took
Leonard Bernstein to turn *Romeo and Juliet* into *West Side
Story* and Cole Porter to transform T*he Taming of the Shrew*
into *Kiss Me Kate*. I've been in neither.

The title role in the upcoming North Coast Theater production of *Sweeney Todd* was off limits, of course, since my performance skills were rusty and it was to be cast with a big-name Equity actor. Also, I was not right for the part unless the show was set in a shtetl and Sweeney was the Hasidic barber of Fleet Street.

I gave up my Actors' Equity union membership and retired as a working stage actor years ago, with no small amount of encouragement from my New York agent. We both found that my looking Jewish was not at all advantageous to my career. I don't mean that I've not been cast because I am Jewish, although earlier in my career I was reminded at the auditions of a regional production of *George M!*—a show about the life and times of musical theater legend George M. Cohan—that the role I was auditioning for was not George M. *Cohen*.

That was at a theater I shouldn't identify called Trinity Playhouse that was run by an artistic director who I can't mention named Christopher Spence.

I have, in fact, often been cast because I looked Jewish, but almost always in small supporting roles in productions penned by Stephen Schwartz, Neil Simon, Paddy Chayefsky and other tribal playwrights writing about the Jewish experience. I've been a bottle dancer in more regional productions of *Fiddler* than I care to remember, and actually played third-Jew-on-the-left in one of the Broadway revivals. I was good, but just not good enough, and so found myself pigeonholed, typecast, and often out of contention.

An ensemble role in *Sweeney Todd* would work just fine for my clandestine operation, and I proposed this to the North Coast Theater's producing artistic director, Andrew Ganz. We met in his ninth-story corner office in The Arcade—a Victorian-era structure within walking distance of the downtown theater district—that was so cluttered with résumés, discarded scripts and theater memorabilia that there was scarcely room for the two of us. Stacks of hard plastic sleeves containing audition DVDs grew from the floor like stalagmites.

Andrew is a tall, lean drink of water with a full head of wavy, insolent light brown hair that manages to find its way into one eye or the other so it can be dramatically swept away. He loved the idea of an actor/critic embedded in one of his productions and the promotional value it would generate. But he reminded me that North Coast Theater was a partnership organization that shared production costs and performances with another theater, and *Sweeney Todd* would be staged and open at the Taos Shakespeare Festival in New Mexico before coming to Cleveland. So unless I was willing to work out of town for a few months, the logistics just wouldn't work out. I was not.

Andrew looked down at the production schedule on his desk and saw that a show earlier in the season, a comedy, would be staged in Cleveland and open in Cleveland, and there were plenty of small roles that I could audition for in just a few weeks. Would I be interested? Perfect, I told him, let's do this.

We shook hands on the deal and Andrew told me that the play was Shakespeare's *As You Like It*.

CHAPTER 3

I Fear Shakespeare

Be not afraid of greatness: some are born
great, some achieve greatness, and some
have greatness thrust upon 'em.

Twelfth Night (Act II, Scene V)

 ERHAPS IT WAS a gross understatement when I suggested that I was not a fan of Shakespeare. It is more of an irrational, overriding, mind-numbing fear.

I don't fear the man, of course, who might not even have written the thirty-nine plays and 154 sonnets attributed to his name. Hundreds of years of speculation by literary scholars and professional naysayers with time on their hands has suggested that playwright Christopher Marlowe, essayist Francis Bacon, dramatist George Peele, adventurer Walter Raleigh, or William Stanley, the 6th Earl of Derby, may well have penned these works, at least in part.

The film *Anonymous*, a 2011 political thriller set in the Elizabethan court, even suggested that a cultured aristocrat named Edward de Vere, the 17th Earl of Oxford, did the writing. He was, in fact, among the most popular of Queen Elizabeth's courtier poets and quite likely her lover. He was also a playwright and the owner of several theater troupes that toured the provinces.

It matters little, for I fear the collective works created in the name of Shakespeare. Intimidated, actually. Overwhelmed. Overwrought. Take your pick. And I am not alone in my trepidation.

An entire website and book series called No Fear Shakespeare is dedicated to deciphering Shakespeare's plays for the flustered, fearful, floundering masses. It puts the original dialogue side by side with a translation into modern, simplified, and supposedly less-dreaded English so the plays are more accessible to the theater-going universe.

According to Duncan Fewins, who lectured at Stratford-upon-Avon College and worked with the Royal Shakespeare Company in the UK, a fear of Shakespeare exists even among the British. "These texts were written 400 years ago and can sometimes appear intimidating. I think that there's still a stigma attached to classical texts: people are still in reverence of Shakespeare," he said in a recent interview.

Yup, my fear is so extreme that I actually find and cite credible sources to confirm its validity. I am a mess.

The thing is, these plays were always difficult to comprehend, even during Shakespeare's lifetime. No one spoke like the plays' characters do in terms of pronunciation and poetry, and they use a vocabulary richer and larger than that employed by the average Elizabethan. Included are words never before spoken by anyone, ever, like "congreeted," which was created to mean "to exchange small-talk pleasantries" and was used only once, only in *Henry V*, and for no apparent reason.

I learned all this from another website, eNotes.com. Its page on "How to Read a Shakespeare Play" opens with this consoling tidbit: "Admit it. You're a little bit scared of Shakespeare. It's a completely understandable response because his plays, after all, are the Mount Everest of English-language literature."

Mount Everest.

That sounds about right. The air gets thinner when I see a Shakespeare play, as if the oxygen in the room has been sucked out by the ghosts of those who attempted and failed to climb to the summit. My brain spins as I try to decipher this incomprehensible text, which at once seems so enticingly familiar yet remains so foreign and always at a distance—like Mount Everest's peak, which exists 8,848 meters above sea level.

I know this because my friend Larry—a soft-spoken, lovable giant of a man and a UC Berkeley-educated therapist—suggested I try to visualize my fear of Shakespeare as a way of conquering it, like patients battling lymphoma. My fear is ice-capped, measures five and a half miles high, and is as expansive as the Himalayan mountain range that straddles Nepal and Tibet.

Larry also told me that clowns, spiders, and public speaking are the most common causes of anxiety and can be debilitating for some. This certainly puts my fear of Shakespeare into proper perspective. I'm looking pretty good when placed on a sliding scale of silly neuroses.

And I pretty much fear the works of Sondheim as well. But that's a whole other precipice.

CHAPTER 4

What Curse

Speak the speech, I pray you, as I pronounc'd
it to you, trippingly on the tongue; but if
you mouth it, as many of our players do, I
had as lief the town-crier spoke my lines.

Hamlet (Act III, Scene II)

*O*F COURSE, MY fear of Shakespeare's plays extends to performing in them.

Over the years I've learned that, within the brotherhood and sisterhood of professional actors, there is a discernible caste distinction between those who earn their living doing Shakespeare and those who do not.

A line seems to have been drawn in the sands of *Twelfth Night's* picturesque beachfront property in Illyria and *The Tempest's* Mediterranean coastline that separates the merely good actors who come and dip their feet in the waters of the classics and the great ones who bathe there. That's me standing on the boardwalk, avoiding getting wet.

It's not like there's a secret handshake among performers proficient in Shakespeare-speak, but there might as well be. They know they have the goods—the ability to make sense of antiquated wordplay and obscure references, the speaking with an Elizabethan cadence and often in rhyme that no longer rhymes, and the capacity to memorize lengthy and complex dialogue and look good doing it—and we know that they know we don't.

Then there are those rarified few who are revered as Master Actors because they have managed to make Shakespeare their bitch. Their legendary reputations have been built squarely on the Bard's broad, canonized shoulders and it has become impossible to hear any one of their names and not free-associate it with his.

Sir Laurence Olivier. Dame Judi Dench. Sir Kenneth Branagh. Sir John Gielgud. Sir Mark Rylance. Sir Ian McKellen. Vanessa Redgrave. Richard Burton. Dame Peggy Ashcroft.

The "Sir" and "Dame" denote the honor of British knighthood bestowed upon those elite English actors who best carry the Bard's banner. This seems a bit pretentious, considering that knighthood used to be awarded solely for military merit and in response to one's faithfulness to the Saviour and the Sovereign. Elton John is also a "Sir." Just saying.

The thought of performing Shakespeare becomes even more daunting when the lead roles have been claimed by knighted luminaries and are forever envisioned in their larger-than-life images. The bar has been set unrealistically high.

As if that is not intimidating enough, shame is bestowed upon those professionals who perform Shakespeare poorly. The unfortunate poster child for such an occurrence is Peter O'Toole. His notorious *Macbeth* performance in 1980 at London's Old Vic Theatre is the stuff that modern myths are made of. Think Richard Dreyfuss's comically pathetic

Off-Off-Broadway portrayal of Richard III in the film *The Goodbye Girl* and double the indignity.

O'Toole's dance with destiny was so bad that the press accused him of single-handedly turning the classic tragedy into a slapstick comedy.

"Chances are he likes the play," wrote Robert Cushman, theater critic for *The National Post*, "but O'Toole's performance suggests that he is taking some kind of personal revenge on it."

According to Michael Billington, theater critic for London's *The Guardian*, "[O'Toole] delivers every line with a monotonous tenor bark as if addressing an audience of deaf Eskimos."

The third performance of the play was stopped by a bomb threat, which was thought by many to be a highlight of the evening, while others found it redundant.

In O'Toole's defense, *Macbeth* is a cursed play. So much so that it is superstitiously referred to as "The Scottish Play" rather than by name by those staging it.

Legend has it that during the very first performance of Shakespeare's bloody masterpiece, on August 7, 1606, at Hampton Court, the young boy scheduled to play Lady Macbeth fell ill and died. The playwright himself had to step into the role. King James was in the audience, took an immediate dislike to the play, and promptly banned it for five years.

During the May 10, 1849, production of *Macbeth* at the Astor Place Opera House in New York City, a simple spat over artistic differences between rival Shakespeare performers Edwin Forrest and William Charles Macready turned into an all-out riot where twenty-two people died and one hundred were injured. The Astor Place Opera House is now a Starbucks.

During a production of *Macbeth* at London's Royal Court Theatre in 1928, the set collapsed upon the first mention of the title character.

And so on.

O'Toole holds the record for the most Academy Award acting nominations without a single win. What curse?

For the past twenty years, I've been the guy panning actors for their poor performances, not the guy getting panned. The thought of being that other guy—of having my name in a press clipping written by a colleague that is as embarrassing and professionally damaging as those just cited and the ones I write—was, quite honestly, frightening.

My therapist friend Larry suggested I read all of Shakespeare's works and read them well. "Overcome the fear, Asher," he advised, "by conquering the work." I read them but have not overcome the fear. Not at all. I simply informed it and, in doing so, exponentially increased my anxiety. I never said Larry was a good therapist.

Still, I've always managed to steer clear of performing in anything remotely Shakespearean and run the risk of getting panned for it. Until now.

CHAPTER 5

Thespian Troupe 44118

What's past is prologue.

The Tempest (Act II, Scene I)

*L*ARRY ALSO SUGGESTED that I attempt to uncover the root cause of my fear so that I can move past it. "Surely," he said late one evening while at the house for dinner with my wife Patty and me, "there must have been a very early encounter with something Shakespearean that is the source of your anxiety. Maybe as a baby you were frightened by a jester at a Renaissance faire."

"I can't imagine my parents ever going to a Renaissance faire. Too many mead-impaired Maid Marians and funnel cakes for their taste. Too much jousting."

"Perhaps as a teenager you were turned down for a date by a girl named Ophelia."

Not a girl and not a date, but the time was October 1982 and the place was the massive proscenium stage in my high school's 1,000-seat auditorium. I was attracted to the stage by all the cute girls who did the spring musical as well as the intriguing proposition of skipping afternoon study hall for play rehearsals. Plus my buddies—a motley collection of second-string athletes and staunchly committed non-joiners—dared me to audition.

So I tried out for the winter drama.

Macbeth.

Full of confidence grounded in blind ignorance, I asked to read for the role of Macbeth, the Scottish general who is manipulated by an ambitious wife and led astray by the prophecies of three evil witches. Afterward, I was asked to read for Macduff, the Scottish nobleman who is hostile to Macbeth's kingship, and then Banquo, the noble general who is killed by Macbeth's murderers because his children, according to the witches' prophecy, are to inherit the Scottish throne.

I was cast as the third murderer.

This role was so small that the character had no name. He was merely a nondescript murderer and the third of three who had no name, so he was actually a lesser murderer. He appeared in one scene only, late in Act III of the five-act play when Banquo is killed. My guy had six lines. They were:

"Macbeth." This is said in response to the first murderer asking the third murderer who he was sent by. Even the other murderers have no clue who the hell he is. He just sort of shows up uninvited, like a distant third cousin at a wedding.

"Hark, I hear horses." This is said to add drama to Banquo's arrival.

"Almost a mile; but he does usually—so all men do—from hence to the palace gate make it their walk." This line refers to the fact that Banquo will probably be walking, rather than riding. Why the third murderer—an uneducated, unnamed, no-account assassin-for-hire—doesn't simply say that Banquo will probably be walking is one of the many things that I find so infuriating about Shakespeare. Even No Fear Shakespeare, the website that translates Shakespeare's English into modern language, had trouble breaking this line down into something less wordy and more comprehendible: "It's almost a mile to the palace gate, but Banquo, like everybody else, usually walks from here to the palace." Yup, much better.

During the three performances of *Macbeth* done by my high school's Thespian Troupe, this line never came out of my mouth the same way twice. My absolute incompetence could very easily have undermined the integrity of the entire play if not for the fact that this line is as inconsequential as it is incoherent. Yet, my ineptitude always pissed off the other murderers, who were no more skilled than I and easily thrown off their game by never quite knowing whether, how, or when this line would make itself known.

"Tis he" was my fourth line. This is said upon Banquo's entrance onto the stage, and so it's redundant and absolutely unnecessary. Still, I said it with gusto, since our director—a twenty-something English teacher and girls JV lacrosse coach—informed us minor players that "every line is a gift that you are giving to the audience."

Line number five was "Who did strike out the light?" There was no light to strike out in our production, since it was a hazard as determined by the Ohio State Fire Marshal, so this line never made sense. Four decades later, there are probably audience members living their otherwise normal lives who wake in the middle of the night and wonder silently what light was being referenced in that high school production of *Macbeth*.

My final line, "There's but one down. The son is fled," is actually a huge responsibility for a novice actor. Banquo's son Fleance escapes after his father is slain by the murderers, which sets significant actions in motion. It's a pivotal line. What a shame I never said it.

With only six lines to say and having to wait nearly two hours into the production to say them, I had a lot of free time backstage while all the other actors were busy performing. During dress rehearsal I discovered how a scar made from just a touch of make-up putty above my right eye and a slight limp in my left leg could make all five feet, six inches and 145 pounds of me look more like a badass assassin. The murder scene took place on a high wooden scaffold built onto the stage that was accessed by a steep flight of stairs.

On opening night, while waiting just offstage for my cue, the putty started melting under the hot lights. By the time I climbed the stairs and blurted out my first line, "Macbeth," I was blind in my right eye and could taste the liquid putty running down my cheek and chin. The other actors in the scene could not stop looking at it.

Preoccupied with what was happening on my face, I barely remember saying my second line, although I do remember royally screwing up the third. The inane "Tis he" came out just fine, as did the confounding "Who did strike out the light?" But when I needed to kill Banquo before my sixth and final line, I had no sense of perspective with only one eye operational and misjudged the distance between us. Awkwardly swinging my heavy blunted blade, I stumbled and fell down the steep flight of stairs, gaining momentum with each step. When the back of my shiny faux chain mail costume made contact with the polished wood floor of the stage, I slid about eight feet and disappeared into the orchestra pit.

By the time I gathered myself and climbed back onto the

stage, Banquo was dead by another's hand and my final line was usurped by the opportunistic second murderer.

So pleased that I did not fall down the stairs and off the stage during the second night's performance—both the limp and the putty were a thing of the past—I completely forgot to say "There's but one down. The son is fled." I just looked down at Banquo's dead body with immense satisfaction as the play—after a pause—went on without me.

So traumatized was I by the third and final performance that my lips moved to deliver this line but no words came out, as if I was whispering sweet nothings to Fleance as he disappeared into the cold, misty Scottish night.

"And what was the reaction after the opening night performance was over?" asked Larry as I finished retelling this long-forgotten piece of my past. By now his huge yeti body was leaning so far forward in his chair that I feared it would topple over.

"I remember that it took me a while to leave backstage because I had to pluck all that coagulated putty from my hair. I lost half my right eyebrow in the process. My parents met me in the auditorium lobby and said I was brilliant and acted as if they were proud, but I don't come from a family of actors. My friends made good-natured fun of me, said they appreciated the Wilhelm scream I let out as I fell off the stage, and suggested I never do acting again. Ever."

"Go on," probed Larry, transitioning from friend to therapist and sensing an aha moment in the making. Following her instincts, Patty got up to find a bottle of single malt scotch and poured some into three glasses.

"The show's director never spoke to me again until graduation day, which was an impressive feat since I was only a junior. And in one of his classes. After the graduation ceremony, he came up to me and asked if I knew what I wanted to study in college. When I said journalism, he seemed relieved."

"Consider yourself fortunate," said Larry.

"Really?" I murmured while reaching for a glass from Patty.

He explained that, for many adults, marriages are ruined, AA meetings are required, and—as was the case with Tommy DeNardo, the fellow who played the second murderer—jail time is allocated because, in high school, they were tortured by upper-class bullies in the locker room or subjected to cruel and highly public practical jokes in the lunchroom. "Many of my patients have had their paths detoured and rerouted," he added, "by simply being the wrong person at the wrong place at the wrong time with the wrong group of high school friends."

"You," he said while accepting a glass of scotch and leaning back in his chair, "simply fear Shakespeare."

CHAPTER 6

Mount Everest

But, for my own part, it was Greek to me.

Julius Caesar (Act I, Scene II)

WHEN ANDREW GANZ, the North Coast Theater's producing artistic director, told me that the play I could audition for was *As You Like It*, it felt as if the oxygen left the room.

My ears started to ring, my head spun as if concussed, and an elephant sat on my sternum.

I grinned at Andrew, nodded and grunted out my thanks like Paleolithic man, and left as quickly as I could under these altered atmospheric conditions. One plodding step after another had become a monumental task.

Once outside the office and on the street, I heard the high-pitched staccato of a little girl's whimper, looked around to find the source, and realized it was coming from me.

I walked toward the outdoor lot where I had parked and the world twirled out of control. I sensed that people were staring at me as I wove and whimpered my way down the sidewalk, and every one of them looked like Peter O'Toole.

They were spouting words in Shakespeare-speak and

none of it made sense to me. They were smiling widely, but they were not amused.

Not in the least.

CHAPTER 7

Run

Boldness be my friend! Arm me, audacity.

Cymbeline (Act I, Scene IV)

AFTER NEARLY THIRTY years of marriage, Patty recognizes that look in my eyes as I come through the front door and face-plant on the living room couch upon my return from Andrew Ganz's office. She hears the muffled whimper and knows enough to walk toward me slowly, quietly, and with a stiff drink in her hands. The drink is for her.

She sits, sips, and says, "So, Asher, what's it this time?"

It is common knowledge among my family and closest friends that I have a tendency to place myself in precarious situations. Worse, I lack the natural instinct to flee once in them. Instead, I fight and never back away. Larry, my therapist friend, calls this the "Napoleon Complex." My high school principal, whose office was my second home and frequent detention center, called it "Short Man Syndrome." My penchant for compensating for my small stature was first recognized by a Pop Warner youth football coach, who made me a running back and used to yell: "Kaufman, try running around those big guys and not through them. You've got your head up your ass." Sounds about right.

I tell Patty about George Plimpton's *Paper Lion* inspiring my auditioning for *Sweeney Todd*. I tell her about *Sweeney Todd* becoming *As You Like It*. I describe how my irrational fear of Shakespeare took the form of sneering Peter O'Tooles accosting me on the street outside the Hedley Theatre, the way all those Mr. Smiths attacked Neo in a park in the second *Matrix* sequel. "At least they weren't spiders or clowns," she says with a smile.

Patty, who would be played by Gwyneth Paltrow in my movie, doesn't fear spiders or clowns or Shakespeare. Or much of anything, save falling.

She cannot drive over an expansion bridge if she can't see beyond its highest point. She is afraid that the car will plummet into whatever body of water is being traversed. Patty is bright. Patty is logical. She is a vice president at a global corporation and can handle pressure like no one else I know. But we need to change seats if she is driving and approaching a bridge. As we cross, she covers her eyes with her shaking hands and envisions facing Poseidon's wrath as our white Prius sinks down through the cold, murky depths of whatever bucolic river, gentle stream, or dried-up tributary we happen to be over. And she nervously hums something tuneless while doing so. Everyone has a thing, it seems, that terrifies them.

"So why don't you just not do this project?" she asks. "Just walk away." I tell her that I can't, for the same reason I can't walk away from a bar fight or a hate crime or that time I was ambushed on national television.

This last one is actually worth recounting.

It was 1995 and I was representing the *Chronicle* as a guest panelist at a journalism conference on the Cleveland College campus. Something clever and quotable I said about the sad state of TV talk shows and how they were passing themselves off as viable news sources made it into the local newspaper, which was picked up by the wire services and seen in a New York newspaper by a producer at *The Phil Donahue Show.*

At the time, exploitative tabloid talk shows bearing the names of their hosts—*Maury Povich, Susan Powter, Richard Bey, Montel Williams, Ricki Lake*—were all the rage. A mainstay on daytime television, each syndicated episode of *The Phil Donahue Show* attracted between five million to fifteen million viewers. The producer called my editor and asked if I was willing to come on the show to discuss tabloid television. I would be one of several guests that represented all facets of the journalism industry. I reminded Mark that I wasn't a "journalist" journalist, just a budding arts reporter and critic. So he told her I would love to do it and she said she would follow up with a date and arrange my transportation to New York City for the taping.

I picked up the local TV schedule to see when *The Phil Donahue Show* aired, but also to get a better sense of the tabloid TV landscape we would be discussing. Today's *Geraldo* featured "women who sleep with married men" while *Sally Jessy Raphael* discussed "disgusting sisters," followed by an hour about homophobia on *Jerry Springer*, featuring gay men coming out to their bowling league, gun club, and church social group.

As one of the original syndicated daytime talk show hosts, Phil Donahue was known for taking the high road. *The Phil Donahue Show*, which originated as a local broadcast in Dayton, Ohio, burst onto the national scene in 1970 by exploring a range of women's issues and pushing the envelope on health and social topics previously considered taboo, like toxic shock syndrome. By the mid-1980s, media critics suggested that the program was running out of relevant ideas, citing a second episode about men wearing skirts as evidence. "He's nearly desperate enough to devote a show to hearing-impaired transsexual Communists," noted *People* magazine. By the 1990s, as the more exploitative shows increased in number and received high ratings, *The Phil Donahue Show* turned completely to the dark side.

Yet here it was doing a straight show about a serious topic.

Two weeks before the taping date I was given, the producer called to tell me that Phil no longer liked the topic, fearing that it was too close to home and the panelists might start targeting his own show on his own show. The topic had been changed to the state of network television news, and although this had nothing to do with what I had said on the Cleveland College campus, was I "all right with that?"

"Run," said the little voice in my head, which I have learned to ignore.

Sure, I said. I am no expert on the topic, so I chatted with friends and acquaintances who were. That way I could sound smart during the very few times I would open my mouth on the program while allowing the other panelists to do the heavy lifting. Patty picked out my clothes so I could look good. I was flown to a hotel in Manhattan and, the next morning, was brought by limo to the NBC studio where Multimedia Entertainment taped the program before an audience.

I was ushered to the Green Room, a well-appointed waiting area, where I met the show's other guests. I knew none of them but had heard of them all: David Bartlett, president of the Radio-Television News Directors Association and spokesperson for the industry; Jerry Nachman, vice president of News at WCBS-TV and former editor-in-chief of the *New York Post*; and Emily Rooney, senior producer at Fox News.

These people personified the network television news industry, high-powered movers and shakers all. They all knew each other and my entrance into the Green Room did nothing to disrupt their lively conversations, warrant any kind of acknowledgment, or inspire introduction.

"Run," my inner voice said with a greater sense of urgency.

They looked agitated and hungry in their expensive suits which, I have since learned, is the natural resting face for TV news executives. When the producer came into the room to welcome everyone, I took her aside and told her I felt outnumbered and outgunned. Not to worry, she said, Phil will keep things balanced. He always does. "He's on your side," I was told with a wink from dead blue eyes.

"Head for the exit and run," said my head.

Just before we were to walk into the TV studio, a half-dressed Phil Donahue burst into the Green Room and announced that the topic has been changed. Connie Chung, who hosted the news magazine *Eye to Eye with Connie Chung* on CBS, had interviewed then-Speaker of the House Newt Gingrich's mom, who had said after some coaxing that her boy Newty "thought [First Lady] Hillary Clinton was a bitch." CBS News aired the segment last night and, said Phil, "Connie, along with all professional journalists, are being harshly chastised by media critics (he looks at me) and heads of journalism programs." That interview and the reaction to it will be today's topic on *The Phil Donahue Show*. "See you in five minutes."

"Run."

The night before, while eating dinner alone and in my underwear in my hotel room with the TV on in the background, I overheard something about Connie Chung and something about Hillary Clinton. I was too lost in my complimentary steak, fries, and side salad to pay much attention. David, Jerry, and Emily, on the other hand, knew about this story the moment it broke and, as industry leaders, had been responding to it throughout the day's news cycle.

With a studio full of tourists with nothing better to do in the city that never sleeps than be an audience for a talk show, the cameras were rolling, and it did not take long before the battle lines were drawn and the war began. Phil thought Connie's line of questioning was appropriate, that the "bitch" comment was worthy of national attention, and that critics and journalism professors did not know what they were talking about. David, Jerry, and Emily laughed at the folly of critics and journalism professors and nodded in agreement as Phil's face, getting increasingly red and puffy, turned to me for a response. I had, it seemed, been promoted from arts journalist at a weekly newspaper to Head Media Critic of the Free World and Dean of All Journalism Programs in the Known Universe during the short walk from the Green Room.

I wished Patty had chosen a darker-colored suit, since this light one under these bright studio lights beautifully showcased the sweat stains that were rapidly spreading from all points north and south.

I could have run. After all, this show wasn't being broadcast live. I could have asked for time out and requested that this program start over and be done without me. I could have stood up, ripped off my microphone, and stormed out the studio door, with no one noticing but a shocked audience, three victorious news executives, one pissed living-dead producer, and a puffy Phil Donahue.

Instead, I stood my ground. I told them and the 8.1 million people who tuned in when the show aired two days later exactly what I thought about Connie Chung, what little I knew about her questionable interviewing tactics, and what I felt about the current state of broadcast journalism. I explained why I thought it. Run? Oh, I don't think so.

Of course, veins full of adrenaline and testosterone have kept me from remembering a thing I said, but I do recall the audience applauding after I said it. I can still see Phil Donahue's piercing eyes penetrating my skull during the show and tearing up afterward as he thanked me and the others profusely for coming. He said it was a really good show and it felt great to get back to serious subjects. He autographed an unsolicited glossy headshot for me and patted me on the back on the way out.

At the time, Phil did not know that he would be off the air by the end of the season, ending a twenty-six-year run on daytime television. Apparently attracting over eight million people was simply not attractive enough in this era of tabloid journalism.

David Bartlett did not know that he would soon be stepping down from his position as president of the Radio-Television News Directors Association after disagreements with its Washington-based board. He took a job as an expert in crisis communications which, by then, he most certainly was.

Emily Rooney, who is the daughter of long-time *60 Minutes* commentator Andy Rooney, did not know that she would soon leave Fox News and host her own TV talk show,

Beat the Press, which criticized—wait for it—the media's coverage of big issues.

Jerry Nachman—the most antagonistic member of the panel, who seemed to have a genuine dislike for Phil and an immediate disdain for me—did not know that he would pass away just a few years later at the age of fifty-seven.

As for Connie Chung, she stepped down from her news magazine shortly after the Mrs. Gingrich interview. She was soon fired as co-anchor of *CBS News with Dan Rather*, jumped to ABC News, and, eventually, stepped out of the limelight. She is married to daytime talk show host Maury Povich, which I find ironic. Connie and Maury probably do not.

As a sidenote, the topic of discussion on Maury's show the day my episode of *The Phil Donahue Show* aired was "Is My Wife Having An Affair With My Son?" Quite the banner day for the Chung/Povich household.

When *The Phil Donahue Show* episode aired, I watched it with Patty and the kids in our living room.

My son, Austin, who was nine at the time, wanted to know why everyone was mad at me and why the guy with all the white hair was always yelling.

My daughter, Zoey, who was five, sat on the floor and hugged my leg for dear life for the duration of the program. I think she was just confused about how I could be in the house and on TV at the same time. Years later she admitted that she held onto me to stop my body from trembling so badly. I had no idea I was trembling. I wonder if she now has an irrational, overriding, mind-numbing fear of daytime talk show hosts.

After we watched, Patty asked why I didn't just walk away—a question she never asked again, until today.

I wanted to say that staying was simply the right thing to

do. That it is important to not back down from adversity and to meet difficult challenges and boisterous bullies head-on. And I wanted to say that facing your fears—like the horror of going on national television as an expert armed with just a sweaty suit and a smile—is the first step in disarming those fears. Going on *The Phil Donahue Show* was the equivalent of confronting clowns, handling spiders, and driving across bridges with eyes wide open.

And, now that I think about it, it's the reason for performing in *As You Like It*. It's so the fear doesn't win.

Instead, I said that it was because I am small in stature and have my head up my ass. And that is what we little people do.

CHAPTER 8

The Chronicle

I am a Jew. Hath not a Jew eyes?

The Merchant of Venice (Act III, Scene I)

*A*BOUT THE *Cleveland Jewish Chronicle.*
The paper was given its name in 1957, but it was the successor to *The Jewish Herald*, which was established in 1907, and the *Hebrew News*, which was founded in 1885 during an upsurge in Jewish immigration in Northeast Ohio.

Originally the paper catered to the immigrant population, addressing relevant issues within a conservative and often Orthodox Jewish perspective. The first few editions were in Hebrew and English.

The paper continues to be Jewish-centric in its focus and mission, but its orientation has gotten increasingly reformed and, some would say, more secular in order to attract a larger and broader readership. And so it includes a sports section despite the remarkable scarcity of Jewish athletes in Cleveland to profile and an entertainment section that covers the visual and performing arts whose works are not necessarily created by, about, or featuring anyone Jewish.

As the theater critic, I cover everything staged by the city's professional companies. The hub of downtown Cleveland's theater scene is Playhouse Square, located on Euclid Avenue between East 14th and East 17th streets. Five theaters and their grand entrance halls were constructed there in the early 1920s, and are lavishly adorned with Italian marble, Czechoslovakian crystal chandeliers, expensive woods, fifty-foot murals, tapestries, and gilded plaster reliefs. Most closed and were ravaged by 1969 during the industrial decline and suburban flight endured by all Rust Belt cities and were set to be razed until a grassroots effort saved the theaters and found the seed money for their eventual renovation, which helped revitalize the downtown area. Playhouse Square now houses eleven stages with more than 10,000 seats.

There's also a thriving professional theater scene consisting of smaller stages on the outskirts of the city. Some, like Dobama Theatre in Cleveland Heights on the east side, are modeled after New York's Off-Broadway and Off-Off-Broadway theaters, which began in the early 1950s as a reaction to the commercial theater that dominated the midtown area. Others, including the nomadic Theater Ninjas, are like the homegrown theaters in Chicago that emerged during the 1960s and 1970s and perform in unorthodox and inexpensive settings away from the mainstream venues in the city's downtown Loop area. Still others, such as convergence-continuum in Tremont and Cleveland Public Theatre in Gordon Square, on the near west side, resemble the 99-seat theaters that evolved in Los Angeles during the '80s, when many of the larger, non-profit professional theaters found themselves dependent on box office sales for most of their income and less likely to engage in creative risk-taking.

While I cover everything, plays and musicals created by artists with last names like Gershwin, Mamet, and Styne are given priority in terms of column inches in the *Chronicle*.

And I am always asked to find a "Jewish angle" and see things through a "Jewish lens," if possible, in what I write. So if there are Jewish artists involved in any way with a production, I am obligated to call them out as a Jewish artist, just like how Adam Sandler's hilarious "Hanukkah Song" calls out famous people who are Jewish and those we think are Jewish but are not.

"O.J. Simpson? Not a Jew."

In doing so, I've discovered that my Semitic radar is not very accurate, which tends to result in a stream of letters to the editor spanking me for my ignorance. Who knew that lyricist Oscar Hammerstein II was Episcopalian and director Norman Jewison was Protestant? And Canadian.

The *Chronicle*, like most newspapers these days, is woefully understaffed. The newsroom is shared by a dozen overworked and underpaid full-time reporters and freelance stringers, half as many columnists who offer opinion or advice, and a handful of highly opportunistic and underqualified journalism interns who are tasked with covering the beats of reporters on vacation, on assignment, or on maternity or medical leave. Gwen, an exceptionally bright and eager-to-please sophomore from a private Jesuit university, has been assigned to me for a few hours a week ever since that whole Hammerstein and Jewison debacle. She is tasked with reading over my copy and coordinating press tickets for my reviews, but I know she is hoping that I get hit by a car so my column will be hers.

Although my editor Mark gives me free rein on the productions I review, he asks that I not cover Christmas shows, touring productions of *Jesus Christ Superstar* and *Godspell*, or stagings of *Cats*. There is nothing particularly Christian about *Cats*; Mark just hates the musical. I often call him

Rum Tum Tugger just to piss him off. And do so with a thick Yiddish accent to show that I can view the world through a Jewish lens.

CHAPTER 9

Damn Shakespeare

God has given you one face, and
you make yourself another.

Hamlet (Act III, Scene I)

*T*HE TIME HAS come to find a role to audition for, one
that is small enough to be manageable but substantial
enough to make my stage time worth writing about.

I'm familiar with *As You Like It*, having binge-read all of
Shakespeare's plays in the quiet solitude of the local library
on the learned advice of my therapist friend Larry. "Conquer
the text," he recommended while pulling pop psychology
out of the ether, "and you'll conquer your fear."

I know the play's basic plot and I can recall its main
characters, but no one pays much attention to the smaller
players, so I really have no idea what my acting options
are. I go online to retrieve a CliffsNotes version of the play,
since my bookshelves at home are a Shakespeare-free zone
for the same reason there are no scenic photographs within
Patty's sightline of Maryland's expansive Bay Bridge, south-
ern France's towering Millau Viaduct, or Tampa's Sunshine
Skyway decorating our walls.

The play is set in a forest, where Duke Senior, his friends, and his supporters decide to reside after leaving the deception and corruption of the court under the tyrannical rule of his brother, Duke Frederick. He is soon joined by his daughter Rosalind and her best friend Celia, who is the daughter of bad Duke Frederick.

Rosalind dresses as a man for the journey in order to avoid being targeted by thieves and because this is what Shakespeare does to female lead characters in his comedies. He does this to Julia in *The Two Gentlemen of Verona*. He does this to Viola in *Twelfth Night*. By doing so, Shakespeare creates the opportunity to offer commentary on gender roles and sexuality within the safe confines of a fictitious and funny storyline. Since men played all the female parts anyway, I suppose it wasn't much of a stretch for a guy to play a girl playing a guy. Elizabethan erotica, if you ask me.

Also heading for the forest is the earnest and handsome Orlando, who is one of two brothers living under Duke Frederick's rule who argue over the rightful inheritance of their deceased father. Rosalind falls in love with Orlando, and he with her. Except, unknown to Orlando, she is a woman impersonating a man. Yup, Elizabethan erotica.

In the mix, though barely, is a minor character named Adam.

The CliffsNotes summary suggests that Adam was the servant of Orlando's now-deceased father, became the servant of Orlando's nasty older brother Oliver by default, and offers to not only accompany the young master into exile but to fund their journey with his modest life's savings. He is a model of loyalty and devoted service. He is way older than everyone else in the play. He is in only four short scenes out of the play's twenty-five scenes across its five acts. He is dying. This I can do.

The website also offers the option of listing each line of dialogue in *As You Like It* for each member of the dramatis personae, so I type in "Adam." He has only ten lines. Nice. Most are brief and end with a series of dots, suggesting that the lines are interrupted by someone more significant with more important things to say and do. Short, sweet, and succinct Shakespeare. As I like it.

I phone Andrew Ganz at North Coast Theater to see if the small role of Adam is on the table. It is. I ask if he would be willing to consider me for it at auditions. He will, adding that William Shakespeare himself acted the role during the play's premiere production.

"Good to know," is about all I can muster amid the brief pang of anxiety this little nugget of historical insight produces.

After our chat I go back to the website to print out the character's ten lines of dialogue so I can start learning them in preparation for the audition. Adam's first line is "Yonder comes my master, your brother" in the very first scene in the first act of the play, while chatting with Orlando. Outside of the pressure of kick-starting the play, this line offers no particular challenges.

"Sweet masters, be patient; for your father's remembrance, be at accord," he says later in the scene while trying to break up the fighting brothers. Again, no problem—a simple and singular line, free of poetry or complexity or rhyming of any kind.

And then old Adam disappears for a while. Five scenes later and early in Act II, Adam overhears Oliver's plot to kill his brother. In an attempt to keep Orlando from entering the house where henchmen lie in ambush, the CliffsNotes indicate that he simply says: "What, my young master? O

my gentle master . . ." But when I click on the line, this is
what gets printed:

> What, my young master, O my gentle master,
> O my sweet master, O you memory
> Of old Sir Rowland! Why, what make you here?
> Why are you virtuous? Why do people love you?
> And wherefore are you gentle, strong, and valiant?
> Why would you be so fond to overcome
> The bonny prizer of the humorous duke?
> Your praise is come too swiftly home before you.
> Know you not, master, to some kind of men
> Their graces serve them but as enemies?
> No more do yours. Your virtues, gentle master,
> Are sanctified and holy traitors to you.
> Oh, what a world is this when what is comely
> Envenoms him that bears it!

"Envenoms him that bears it," indeed.

And so it goes for the remaining seven lines. Apparently,
the dots at the end of the sentences don't signify interrup-
tion or the character trailing off as if lost in reverie; they
denote continuation. One sentence on my computer screen
becomes many on the printed page. Most of Adam's short
lines, it seems, are lengthy mouthfuls of prose with a smat-
tering of poetry. Damn Shakespeare.

Staring down at pages of printed text, flop sweat surfaces
as I quickly realize that I am going to need some help getting
through all the Elizabethan verbiage that has been assigned
to poor, old, insignificant, dying Adam. How do I memorize
this stuff? How do I even comprehend it? What's the trick
to getting these convoluted words from page to stage during

the audition? I am pretty clueless and already anxious. And the air is thinning.

My experience as a local critic has connected me with all the artistic directors of Cleveland area theaters that do Shakespeare. I've reviewed the best actors who perform there.

Auditions are just around the corner. Time to call in some chips.

CHAPTER 10

Critics Are Hated and So Excoriated

If you prick us, do we not bleed?
If you tickle us, do we not laugh?

The Merchant of Venice (Act III, Scene I)

W HO AM I kidding? Critics have no chips to call in or cash. Hell, most critics have no friends.

It is easy to lose whatever friends you have when all your Friday and Saturday nights are either spent at the theater without them or they are dragged to share an evening of bad theater. And sitting in the dark for two hours is most certainly not the place to make new friends. It is also nearly impossible for a critic to make friends within the arts community.

The relationship between most theater critics and actors, directors, designers, and administrators is cordial but most certainly tenuous and tentative. This is due to the unhealthy underlying professional co-dependence that defines it. A critic's review is based solely on the work of theater artists and technicians. A theater's success—that is, box office sales, promotional campaigns, a playwright's prominence, and an actor's reputation—are all influenced by a critic's review.

This makes for an awkward, imbalanced, and parasitic relationship, and not lasting friendship.

How awkward?

In the lobby just before an opening night production, an obligatory hello, hug, or handshake takes place between the arriving critic and greeting theater management. This is followed by a brief conversation. It's a professional courtesy, really, for no artistic director or publicist wants to appear to be kissing up to a critic, and no critic wants to give them an opportunity to do so. Linger a little too long or laugh a little too loud and it feels odd to everyone concerned.

These encounters in the atrium are over before they even begin.

During the performance, critics can feel the penetrating eyes of the director locked on the backs of their heads from the rear of the theater, looking for tell-tale signs of a positive or negative reaction. I'm convinced that my hair is thinner back there, seared from the staring.

Intermission is an exercise in evasion, with both parties avoiding each other for fear that body language will give away their respective impressions on how the production is going. The restroom is typically off-limits for critics. My greatest nightmare is being stuck in a urinal adjacent to ones occupied by the playwright and a producer and having to seem too preoccupied with peeing to look up and engage in potentially revealing conversation.

After a performance, critics habitually sidle out of their aisle seats during applause, scuttle to the back of the house, and sulk while exiting the theater like hunted, haunted animals, avoiding all eye contact while doing so. They lurch out into the darkness and disappear into the cold, dark night. Only superheroes make more dramatic exits, although they do so with no greater sense of urgency, mission, or self-importance.

There is often a catered meet-and-greet with the cast and director after an opening night performance, which is intended for family, friends, financial backers, and season subscribers. And by catered, I mean sparkling wine, cheese cubes, and tiny, tasteless pastries. Critics are invited as well, but I always felt that doing so undermined the whole superficial handshake in the lobby/bathroom avoidance/caped crusader escape out the back and into the night ritual.

Therein lies another reason why critics have no friends, for any friend accompanying a critic on opening night would love to linger in the lobby, have some snacks, and chat about the show with the cast. I drag my superhero side-kicks kicking and screaming out into the parking lot, pick their brains for their take on the production, and bring them home so I can pour a scotch and start writing a critique.

This long-standing tradition of interpersonal discomfort and mutual distrust repeats itself at every theater at every opening night during every season.

How long-standing?

It is safe to say that Shakespeare had no professional critics in the late-1500s and early-1600s, given the dismal state of newspapers, though he had supporters, sponsors, detractors, and promoters who would publicly compliment or admonish his work. But no one was scuttling out of the Globe Theatre to meet a deadline for the morning edition.

The profession of theater critic was not codified until the 18th century because, quite frankly, there was no great call for it. Newspapers and a large, literate audience to read them did not surface in earnest until well into the 1700s. When it did, those who chose the theater as a profession were not deemed particularly important or sufficiently newsworthy to warrant much attention in the press. Most of the papers of the time concentrated on matters of politics, the church, and the conflict between the two. If the stage was mentioned at all, it was usually within the context of a controversy between the dramatists and the Puritans or the murder of a director by an actor.

In London in the late-1700s, theater critic was an occupation pursued only by what has been described in one historical text as "managerial toadies, managers puffing their own wares, opportunistic knockers [and] unclassified eccentrics."

In the United States at that time, theater criticism was described as "fly-by-night news-sheets and scurrilous pamphlets popping up everywhere, mingling blind-item theatrical gossip with detailed analysis, often willfully and malevolently inaccurate, of plays and performances."

It's been argued that not much has changed.

One thing that has is the weight given to what a critic writes. In the most theater-centric cities in the country with access to the most powerful publications in the world, critics have been an elite corps of tastemakers and culture shapers. It's been suggested that, among New York critics, Broadway is believed to be a kind of theatrical Citadel and their job is to keep the barbarians from the gates. Feelings are hurt, reputations are tarnished, and investments are nullified by a negative review. Critics often mold the arts by pushing artists to raise the bar on the quality of their writing, the nature of their performance, or the amount of risk being taken in their productions.

Of course, sometimes the artists push back. Literally.

The New York Herald Tribune critic Walter Kerr was physically thrown from the Public Theater by producer and director Joseph Papp after a particularly negative review in the 1960s.

In 1973, in a New York restaurant, actress Sylvia Miles—best known at the time for playing a hooker for six minutes in the film *Midnight Cowboy*—dumped a plateful of food on *New York* magazine critic John Simon's head after an unflattering review of her performance in *Nellie Toole and Co*. Simon, ever the stickler for details, noted that the plate consisted of pâté, steak tartare, brie, and potato salad.

Cleveland has not been exempt from such bad behavior, even though the market is smaller than New York and the critics are less powerful. In 2006, then-theater critic Tony Brown wrote a negative review of the Cleveland Play House's production of *Rabbit Hole* for the city's only daily paper, *The Plain Dealer*. During a nasty curtain speech at a subsequent production, then-artistic director Michael Bloom called out the critic in the crowd. When Bloom walked out of the theater after the speech, Brown was close behind. The two met in the lobby and the artistic director took a swipe at the critic but missed, much to the chagrin of the season ticket holders who were hoping for a better fight.

Sometimes the pushback from artists takes a more creative, passive-aggressive turn.

As if he were anticipating adversity from the critics, playwright Samuel Beckett makes that profession the most grievous insult among the many exchanged between the two main characters in his avant-garde play *Waiting for Godot*:

VLADIMIR: Moron!
ESTRAGON: Vermin!
VLADIMIR: Abortion!

ESTRAGON: Morphion!
VLADIMIR: Sewer Rat!
ESTRAGON: Curate!
VLADIMIR: Cretin!
ESTRAGON [with finality]: Crritic!

In plays and films that feature an arts critic as a central character, that individual is, more often than not, provided with the wittiest dialogue but nastiest persona. Look no further than George S. Kaufman and Moss Hart's 1939 classic *The Man Who Came to Dinner*, where the famously pompous critic and radio personality Sheridan Whiteside is invited to dine at the house of a rich factory owner, injures his hip after slipping on a patch of ice and makes life a living hell for the household.

A disquieting but not surprising number of characters who are critics are murdered. In the wonderfully campy 1973 film *Theater of Blood*, a Shakespearean actor played by Vincent Price is humiliated by members of the Theatre Critics Guild at a coveted awards ceremony. He sets out to exact vengeance against the nine critics by killing them, one by one, in a manner similar to famous murder scenes from Shakespeare's plays. Just before his character plunges to his death by jumping off of a burning building, Price— who always wanted the chance to perform Shakespeare but found himself typecast because of his work in horror films— gets to deliver the final monologue from the tragedy *King Lear*. He savors the line, "Howl, howl, howl, howl! O, you are men of stones" as the surviving critics look on.

A critic is stabbed to death in the opening act of Ken Ludwig's 2012 whodunit comedy *The Game's Afoot*. A critic is eaten by evil forces in M. Night Shyamalan's 2006 film

Lady in the Water. And in Conor McPherson's 1997 play *St. Nicholas*, a critic is kept alive only to serve as a food forager for vampires. That play is particularly popular in the community theater circuit, which speaks volumes about the relationship between amateur playhouses and the local press.

No, critics have no friends in the theater, and I have no chips.

CHAPTER 11

Casting Call

The fault, dear Brutus, is not in our stars,
but in ourselves, that we are underlings.

Julius Caesar (Act I, Scene II)

*T*HE PHONE RINGS.

"Asher, it's Andrew Ganz. Looking forward to tomorrow?"

"Hi, Andrew. Tomorrow for what?"

"Your audition."

That this appointment never made it into the planner I keep in my office at home or the event calendar on my computer or the alarm function of my phone is, I am sure, just a silly oversight. My therapist friend Larry would probably have a different take on this.

Andrew said that I can have the script with me on stage during my audition, which I will. I had been scouring the Arden Shakespeare version of the script I picked up, reading the 142-page introduction that provides theatrical, cultural, social, and historical context for this play, reading the sidebar commentary, and reading the extensive footnotes.

I learned that *As You Like It* was probably written at the end of 1598, first performed in 1599, and initially printed in the First Folio in 1623. The play provides a "more varied palette of verse forms and prose rhythms than is present in any earlier Shakespeare play," which sent a shiver up my spine. It "touches some of the deepest chords of human experience," writes the author of the introduction, as if warning me to do due diligence while simultaneously pushing all my psychological pressure points.

Old Adam is only mentioned in passing and always in short footnotes. From them I learned that Adam is weak from hunger at the start of the play and starving by Act II. He is so weak that he has to be carried onto the stage late in that act and is dead soon after.

I can play dying and dead, but I find myself still staring at Adam's lines, hoping that their meaning, the proper cadence of their delivery, and the deepest chords of human experience that they may happen to be touching will avail themselves. Nope.

And now I'm wondering if these lines are, in fact, actually incomprehensible because of some dubious edit in the First Folio. Maybe not being able to make heads nor tails of the words I see before me has similarly plagued the minor actors taking on the role for the past 400 years, but they have been too embarrassed to admit it. Or no one will listen. Maybe Andrew knows that casting me in this role is a cruel joke that has been shared by centuries of artistic directors who know that playing Adam will be and always has been an exercise in futility.

The script's introduction suggests that, in Shakespeare's day, people said they went "to hear" his plays. No one said, "I saw *Julius Caesar*," because plays were part of an aural tradition. So I try to speak the words aloud, hoping that their meaning would manifest themselves in the spoken word.

But every attempt at verbalizing Adam's dialogue sounds like a tale told by an idiot, full of sound and fury, signifying nothing.

As I head for the audition, part of me is hoping that the car won't start, that the world will end, or my skull will explode from the tension that has been building since my conversation with Andrew. But the car starts, the world goes about its business, and my pressurized head somehow gets me downtown to the North Coast Theater rehearsal stage.

Andrew has scheduled my audition for the end of the work day, after hours of watching with director Michael Price dozens of skilled professional actors performing lengthy monologues from other classic works and then acting out scenes featuring the characters they hope will be theirs. By the time I arrive, the director and the assistant who has been reading the dialogue of the other characters in the scenes being performed have left for the day. Andrew is making notes, lost in thought and unaware that I have hesitantly taken my place at center stage. So I stand with script in hand and wait.

"Ah, Asher. Old Adam is it? Show me."

I close my eyes and take some increasingly frail breaths so as to get in the elderly character's dying frame of mind.

"Asher, you OK?"

"Sure," I say. "Just need a minute to get into this."

When I open my eyes to begin the audition, Andrew is right next to me on stage, his tall and lanky figure casting shadows in every direction. "I've been sitting for hours," he says, wiping his crazy hair away from his eyes. "How about I read all the other lines from here, so we can move around the stage, improvise a little, have some fun with this."

"Cool."

As I old-man wheeze my first line, "Yonder comes my master, your brother . . . ," Andrew whacks me in the chest with blunt force. I take a step back and instinctively utter, "What the fuck?!" just before he whacks me again and says, as Orlando, "Go apart, Adam, and thou shalt hear how he will shake me up," which is in reference to the entrance of his troublesome brother, Oliver. I can tell immediately that Andrew is one of those who bathe in the waters of the picturesque beachfront property of *Twelfth Night's* Illyria. He's really good.

"Now," instructs a playful and mobile Andrew, who's obviously getting some blood-flow back in his extremities, "try to get between me and my brother, because we are about to go at it."

And so the two of us move about the stage, spewing dialogue—some of it written by Shakespeare—and working our way through the script, one Adam scene after another, as if we were sparring partners. Then Andrew lifts me up in his arms, carries me downstage and lays me on the floor. As he does, I say, "So had you need; I scarce can speak to thank you for myself," which is, I believe, Adam's final line before he dies offstage, unseen and forgotten.

"OK, then," declares Andrew as he stands erect, stares down at me a moment, turns, and then bounds off the stage. He walks toward his audition table and, while scribbling something down, says, "You got the part."

What the fuck?!

CHAPTER 12

Climb Every Mountain

Thus must I from the smoke into the smother.

As You Like It (Act I, Scene II)

OXYGEN RAPIDLY LEAVES the rehearsal space and my ears start to ring as I thank Andrew for the opportunity over the din and stumble toward the exit.

The ring is soon replaced by that high-pitched little girl whimper that I now know belongs to me as I walk out of the building and toward the outdoor lot where I've parked my car.

I take out my phone and reach my editor's office after three failed attempts at pushing the blurry auto-dial button and leave the message that "It's George Plimpton. We're in business."

The Peter O'Tooles have returned and, clutching their devastating press notices, they embrace me like a brother.

CHAPTER 13

Ten Syllables, Five Stressed

We are such stuff as dreams are made on.

The Tempest (Act IV, Scene I)

I'M ON MY way to *As You Like It* rehearsal at the Hedley Theatre in downtown Cleveland and run into ridiculous traffic, rush hour traffic. I look at my watch and see that it's just after 10 a.m., so this tie-up is unusual for this city. And I'm late for rehearsal, which is uncharacteristic of me.

As I veer off the highway and see the theater in the distance, there are cops everywhere who are attempting to control a sea of pedestrians trying to cross the street and head toward the Hedley Theatre as well. So many people! And everyone, coupled and courteous, is dressed to the nines in furs and pearls, tuxes and ties. Flashbulbs are going off and it suddenly occurs to me that tonight is Opening Night! And I'm late.

I abandon my car in the middle of traffic, toss the keys to the nearest cop—who tells me to "break a leg"—and work my way to the theater's rear entrance stage door. Now I'm in a panic. I don't remember rehearsing the play and I certainly don't recall tech rehearsal. And as I pass the theater's marquee, I see that I'm about to appear in Shakespeare's *Troilus and Cressida*.

When I get to the stage door, I'm confronted by the security guard, stewed to the gills and practically falling off his too-small stool. He wags a sausage-like finger at me and says "Come in time! Have napkins enow about you, here you'll sweat for't." He winks at me. "The Porter in *Macbeth*," he says, sensing that I am clueless about those words and their origin.

"Say what?" is my only reply.

"Our knocking has awaked him: here he comes."

Just then, rapidly working his way down the darkened narrow backstage hallway toward the stage door is Andrew Ganz, dressed in traditional Elizabethan garb complete with pumpkin pants, muffin cap, and pointy shoes.

"Where have you been? Aboard, aboard, for shame! The wind sits in the shoulder of your sail, and you are stay'd for."

"Wait—what!?" I say.

"That's from *Hamlet*," he says impatiently, "and we've got to get you into costume now!" He quickly shepherds me through the door, down the hallway, through the crowded wing space where well-known actors in full Shakespeare finery—Emma Thompson, Orson Welles, and John Barrymore—prepare to go on stage. We head back to where an array of costumes on hangers are located. "You've got to take the lead tonight," shouts Andrew. "He fell! O, what a fall was there, my countrymen! Then I, and you, and all of us fell down."

"*Julius Caesar*," says the costumer, who reaches for a hanger and hands me a tunic with a built-in hump just below the left shoulder. She strips me naked and says, "Don't forget your props" as she hands me a stick with a grotesque jester's head and round silver bells jangling from its little cap.

And there I am, naked with a costume from *Richard III* in one hand and a stick in the other, getting ready to enter the cavernous, blindingly lit performance space from stage right to perform the opening scene of *Troilus and Cressida*. The massive purple curtain is closed, but I can hear the muffled chatter of what seems like thousands of impatient subscription ticket holders taking their seats on the other side.

When the chatter rises in volume and becomes the irritating, ear-splitting, and prolonged sound of cicadas that have instinctively returned after years of deep hibernation, I realize that I am dreaming. Strange how being naked, holding a hump, and bumping into Orson Welles in the wings didn't clue me in earlier.

"I'm dreaming," I say with confidence to anyone within earshot.

Walking toward me across the stage is my editor, Mark, who says: "To die, to sleep; To sleep: perchance to dream. *Hamlet.*"

"Really? You too?"

Suddenly I'm standing in bright, overhead silhouette light, and say to Mark:

This isn't funny now; I'm freaking out!
I'm somehow s'posed to know just what to do
with something like a thousand people there
expecting some tragedian to come
deliver them a penetrating speech
of greatest depth, of such poetic truth
so as to leave no eye undimmed with tears!
Instead, they're getting me and all my fears.
I can't speak poetry, for sure not prose.
And I'm not really sure how blank verse goes.

"Well," says Mark, "you've been speaking verse all this time. Ten syllables, five stressed. Been rhyming too. Now, get out there and perform *Troilus and Cressida* as you've never performed it before."

"I've never performed it before."

"There ya go."

The curtain starts to rise as Mark pivots to leave, but he stops halfway, dramatically turns to the now-visible, silent, and very attentive audience, and recites: "Is it not monstrous that this player here, but in a fiction, in a dream of passion, could force his soul so to his own conceit."

"That's from *Hamlet*," shouts the audience in unison.

As I prepare to say my first line as old Adam, I awaken from the fever dream.

It's around 2 a.m. and my sheets have been violently kicked to the far reaches of the bed. I turn on a lamp, grab the pen and paperback collection of Sudoku puzzles on my nightstand, and write down in the margins as much of this insane dream as I can before it fades. Grabbing the phone, I text my friend Larry and ask that he schedule me for a therapy session ASAP. "Come armed with some Sigmund Freud," I type to the accompaniment of Patty's light snoring, "and I'll pick up a few volumes of No Fear Shakespeare."

CHAPTER 14

Let the Healing Begin

How poor are they that have not patience!
What wound did ever heal but by degrees?

Othello (Act II, Scene III)

*L*ARRY IS MY therapist friend, but he is not officially my therapist, so I'm new at this.

When I arrive at the office building that houses his group practice, I am ushered into an outer waiting room already occupied by a small menagerie of internally damaged people awaiting help. Not to cast aspersions, but the anticipation and intensity with which they react to the receptionist opening the door that leads to the therapists' offices and the crestfallen disappointment that follows when it is clear she has come for me suggests that these folks are not bothered by your garden-variety spiders and public speaking. They shoot daggers at me from their eyes as they return to their back issues of *People* magazine.

We walk in silence down a long, carpeted hallway with soothing artwork on the walls—pastoral scenes, mostly—and pass the closed doors of therapists' offices before stopping in front of Larry's. She knocks, the door opens, and Larry meets me at the entrance with a toothy grin and the Sigmund Freud edition Magic 8 Ball I gave him for his last birthday. "Per your request," he says and hands me the novelty toy as the receptionist turns and leaves. I hand over my Sudoku paperback filled with barely legible late-night notation and the No Fear Shakespeare versions of *Hamlet, As You Like It,* and *Troilus and Cressida* I was carrying.

The traditional prognosticating Magic 8 Ball that I remember from when I was a kid has a twenty-sided white die floating in dark blue liquid inside its black, round frame. When asked a question and shaken, a random answer like, "Without a doubt," "My sources say no," and "Reply hazy, try again" is revealed through a small glass window at the base of the orb. The gag gift I gave Larry is a knockoff that offers witty advice loosely grounded in Freud's psychoanalysis. Larry interpreted my not-so-subtle jab at what he does for a living—more guesswork than actual science—as a humorous and thoughtful present. And so I left it at that.

Larry tells me to come in, unaware that his huge, Sasquatch body fills the doorway and makes it impossible to enter. After a moment, he backs away and nods to an oversized, overstuffed chair. As I sit and attempt to find a comfortable position, I look around and notice the wildly abstract and genuinely disturbing framed images that dominate his walls. "Rorschach tests?" I ask. "Artwork by the ex," he says, "which I've been meaning to replace." He walks up to one, looks at it closely, and admits that, though the marriage ended amicably three years ago, he still harbors feelings of anger and loss.

So, yes, Rorschach tests.

Woefully under-watered potted plants with dead, fallen leaves at their base are scattered throughout the office, which does not bode well for a professional caregiver. I don't call attention to them for fear that they will remind Larry of how he still harbors feelings of being ignored and abandoned.

My friend sits down in a big black leather easy chair that faces me, rubs his giant hands together, and declares: "Let the healing begin."

"Normally," he says, "I start by asking patients to talk about what's on their mind, but since I know what's on yours, let's cut to the quick."

"Sounds good."

"Your dream is pretty boilerplate anxiety based on an overwhelming sense of insecurity and vulnerability. That's what the nudity, the showing up for rehearsal but discovering it's opening night, and the expectation of doing a small part in one play and then realizing you will be performing the lead in a different play is all about. That's why everyone but you—even the drunken security guard and your editor—speaks fluent Shakespeare. We've all had dreams similar to this, which take place in our old elementary school, at the office . . . any very public space that holds meaning for us. We're always naked—exposed—and always out of time and place."

While Larry is saying this, I shake the Freud toy, glance down and read its take on my dream: "Sometimes a cigar is just a cigar." Larry, 1; Magic 8 Ball, 0.

"But why is the play I am about to perform in my dream *Troilus and Cressida?*" I ask.

Larry takes a few minutes to read through the first few pages of one of the texts I brought. "Well," he says, "it's apparently Shakespeare's least popular, least produced, and most unsuccessful play. The first half is relatively light-hearted, which is weird for a play set during the Trojan War, and the second half is tragic. But this says that the play doesn't deliver the happy ending expected of a comedy or the feeling of catharsis anticipated at the end of a tragedy." Looking up from the book, he adds, "You have subconsciously put yourself in a problem play so that your failure is not your own, but the playwright's."

"If it's not one thing, it's your mother" is the best the all-seeing, all-knowing Freudian orb can offer. Larry, 2; Magic 8 Ball, 0.

"Why Orson Welles in the wings? That really freaks me out."

He thinks about this for a few beats and shrugs his oversized shoulders. "Damned if I know. Maybe because he did a lot of Shakespeare in his heyday? I remember him doing bad TV commercials for Paul Masson wines toward the end of his acting career. I don't think that Orson Welles in the wings means anything. What does the ball say?"

I shake it and read: "'We will sell no wine before its time.' No, actually, the ball says 'You're in denial!' Not bad. Looks like you've been spanked by a Mattel toy, Therapy Boy."

"Really?! How about I dissect the homoeroticism in every one of these plays?" he asserts while defensively thumbing through the No Fear Shakespeare texts. "Let's see the piece of plastic do that."

Larry, 2; Magic 8 Ball, 1.

"Toward the end of my dream I remember breaking into perfect verse. What's that about?"

"Dreams tend to reveal what is going on subconsciously. You, the real Asher, are terribly insecure about performing Shakespeare's words, but the Asher in your dream," he says while looking down at the notes I scribbled after dreaming, "is not. He says he/you can't speak poetry while speaking poetically, and when he says he/you can't speak in blank verse, the sentences are all ten syllables, five stressed."

"So?"

"Deep down inside you know that you can do this play, speak these words, and find their rhythms. Plus, you are holding a costume that displays an imperfection—a hump— but you're not wearing it."

"And my editor spewing *Hamlet*?"

Again, Larry looks at the remnant of the quote in my notes and then opens up the pertinent No Fear Shakespeare volume to confirm the proper wording of what Mark offered in my dream. He reads the original text from *Hamlet*, Act II, Scene II: "'Is it not monstrous that this player here but in a fiction, in a dream of passion, could force his soul so to his own conceit.'"

Looking at the dumbed-down version on the opposite side of the page, he reads: "'It's awful that this actor could force his soul to feel made-up feelings in a work of make-believe.'"

"Meaning?"

"Well, Asher, what do YOU think it means?" asks Larry, now in full therapist mode.

"It means, why don't I just try acting because Shakespeare has already done the heavy lifting. OK. I get it."

I shake the Magic 8 Ball. This time it actually offers some insightful Sigmund Freud reflection: "Out of your vulnerabilities will come your strength."

I shake it again for confirmation: "The virtuous man contents himself with dreaming that which the wicked man does in life." That's pretty much on target.

Larry, 2; Magic 8 Ball, 3.

CHAPTER 15

Thin Skin

The wheel has come full circle.

King Lear (Act V, Scene III)

*T*HIS AFTERNOON—THE DAY before our first rehearsal—
is the first meeting of the sixteen-member cast, North
Coast Theater artistic director Andrew Ganz, his technical
and administrative support staff, New York-based director
Michael Price, and his team of artistic designers. It will take
place in the cavernous, no-frills-but-well-lit and acoustically
treated rehearsal room buried in a building behind downtown Cleveland's Playhouse Square complex. This will be
our home for the three weeks before *As You Like It* runs tech
rehearsals, soft opens for preview performances, and then
launches into a four-week run at the Hedley Theatre across
the street.

This first contact is meant to give everyone a sense of the
scope of this creative undertaking and introduce all those
involved in achieving its success. It also introduces everyone
to the performance space where the play will be blocked and
rehearsed without scenery, dramatic lighting, costuming, or
most other production elements before we head over to the

Hedley. There will just be tape on the floor to mark where set pieces, the left and right wings, and the edge of the stage will be.

The most important outcome of this meeting is the bonding that needs to take place between the six professional actors who are making their North Coast Theater debut, including me, and the ten standing members of the company. Some of the North Coast regulars have been cast mates for as many as thirteen seasons and they have recently performed together in this season's repertoire of *Love's Labour's Lost* and *Murder on the Nile*. They will be performing in *Sweeney Todd* after *As You Like It* closes. They are a tight-knit group who can finish each other's thoughts and iambic pentameter sentences.

We newbies are strangers to each other and to the North Coast actors, though all the North Coast actors know of me. Their names have appeared in my reviews for years and, yes, I believe I have skewered most of them at one time or another.

Negative reviews are an occupational hazard for artists. Kenneth Tynan, longtime critic for London's *The Observer*, once wrote, "The critic's job—at least nine-tenths of it—is to make way for the good by demolishing the bad." The math is about right, and going negative in reviews has become so normative that sometimes high praise from the critics catches the marketing personnel at theaters off guard. After the campy musical *Xanadu* opened on Broadway, the promotional ads read: "The critics loved it. Seriously."

One of the most notorious theater critics of all time was *The New York Times'* Frank Rich, who earned the moniker "The Butcher of Broadway" for the acidity of his reviews and their ability to kill shows in their tracks. He so dominated the theater scene in the 1980s that if he disliked a play he saw in London, producers would not even bother to bring it to New York. His most lethal review was for the mystery farce *Moose Murders*, which began: "Those of us who have witnessed the play that opened at the Eugene O'Neill Theater last night will undoubtedly hold periodic reunions, in the noble tradition of survivors of the Titanic." The show opened and closed on February 22, 1983.

Demolition is not in my nature. And I've always believed that even if a show goes south, a negative review should at the very least be well-crafted and—to borrow from the Hippocratic Oath—do no harm. But sometimes, when it is late at night and you are staring at a blank computer screen after having spent two and a half hours sitting through a poorly written play or watching actors who lack conviction or witnessing production choices that miss their mark by miles, it's tempting to skip the pleasantries and go right for the jugular.

I once wrote that seeing a particular play was like a "sobering interlude of minimum-security imprisonment," which was aptly rewarded with press tickets for that theater's next production that placed me fifteen rows farther back, to the side and behind someone with a huge head. I've called a show "the musical theater equivalent of Ambien." Just last week, I noted that "when the lights came up at intermission, startled audience members could be seen finishing last Sunday's crossword puzzle." I'm no "Butcher of Broadway," nor would I ever want to be, but once you've taken a walk on the dark side, the path becomes increasingly easy to navigate and the quickest way home.

One of the most negative reviews I've ever written actually landed me the job at the *Chronicle* after I'd been covering the Cleveland theater beat for a different newspaper. It was for a production of *Seussical: The Musical*, which the previous critic at the *Chronicle* adored but the paper's publisher, who was also in the audience, hated. My headline, "Not a Fan I Am," got the publisher's attention and made him curious about what came next, which was:

I am not a big fan of pentameter verse
Gilbert and Sullivan bothers me worse
But the one writing style for which I've no use
Is the preening rhymed scheming of one Dr. Seuss

Seussical is a show full of tales disconnected
From books that Seuss wrote, each one well respected
They are thrown in together and tied to a plot
To give it a flow, but a flow it has not

Playwrights Ahrens and Flaherty are certainly pros
But I don't like their play, it's just one of those shows
Yet Spotlight East Theater thought to give it a try
So review it I will with expectations not high

This musical, which was poorly received and short-lived on Broadway, is populated by creatures called Whos as well as other peculiar citizens of Whoville, including a modest-tailed bird named Gertrude McFuzz who is envious of other birds' plumage. Silvia Cooper, a very serious young actress who was new in town and seemed terribly out of place in such a silly musical, played Gertrude. She did so with sobering dramatic realism, as if the role was written by a 19th century Russian playwright rather than a contemporary American children's book author. I wrote:

There's an ensemble cast, which is not that unusual
And plenty of songs, par for plays that are musicals
But Silvia Cooper as a featured Who-not
Hit all the wrong notes and at all the wrong spots

She plays Lady McFuzz as if penned by Chekhov
Which has audiences yelling "enough is enough"
Oh, she isn't the only one performing like this
But the scale of it makes her so hard to be missed

The 29th of October ends the run of this show
If you're planning on coming that's as far as it goes
But be warned of the impact of seeing this play
It lasts just two hours but it feels like two days

In the upcoming production of *As You Like It,* I will be
sharing the stage with Silvia Cooper, who will be playing
the female lead Rosalind.

Not long ago, I reviewed a comedy called *Legends!* The
play is about two waning and desperate female movie stars
who are coerced into doing a Broadway production. They
deplore each other and, in the Broadway show, will be
playing two waning and desperate movie stars who deplore
each other. The play was created as a touring star vehicle for
theater legends Mary Martin and Carol Channing and, later,
for TV legends Linda Evans and Joan Collins, and it never
got good reviews. Half the audience in attendance at this
local production walked out at intermission. This is something you rarely see in Cleveland, where avid theatergoers
are remarkably charitable and give standing ovations for
just about everything. I've seen audiences stand for a scene
change.

One of the featured actors in this terrible production of this terrible play was Erin Andrews, who was miscast and struggled mightily with the material. In order to give my readers a sense of why the audience bailed at halftime, I likened the show to "an excursion through hell. Third class with a middle seat." More specifically, I selected the nine circles of hell represented in Dante's epic poem *Inferno*. I wrote: "The Seventh Circle, devoted to those who commit violence against art, is where we find Andrews and the strong smell of brimstone she leaves in her wake."

Erin Andrews, who is Silvia Cooper's life partner, will be playing Celia, Rosalind's cousin and best friend, in *As You Like It*.

It gets worse.

I reviewed our director Michael Price's work well before he was brought to Cleveland from New York City for our production. He had spearheaded the national tour of *Summer: The Donna Summer Musical*—a bio-musical about the life, times, and tunes of the late-1970s/early-1980s disco icon—that came through Playhouse Square. Had I known that I would soon be working with the guy in *As You Like It*, I certainly wouldn't have gone all Shakespearean in the review's headline: "Now is the *Summer* of our Discontent."

Mind you, I have written plenty of equally glowing reviews about these folks and the other North Coast actors who will be in this production. But performing artists tend to have remarkable albeit selective memories, and I will find out momentarily which ones also have thin skins.

CHAPTER 16

Meet-and-Greet

I desire you in friendship, and I will
one way or other make you amends.

The Merry Wives of Windsor (Act III, Scene I)

*T*HERE's COFFEE AND a table full of bite-sized snacks at
the meet-and-greet which, along with the absence of
chairs, suggests that this meeting will be brief.

Everyone mingles and the actors engage in casual conversations about mutual colleagues, shared directors, and
stories of being in the same plays performed at different
production houses in cities across the country. All this
starts forming a sense of community among artists who will
become intimately familiar with each other's talents and
trusting of each other's creative choices when we eventually
share space on stage for twenty-five performances.

When I introduce myself by name, I sense that most
of the North Coast actors are more than a little surprised,
apprehensive, and untrusting of me in this first encounter.
Their eyes open wide and they involuntarily take a half-
step back as if regaining balance from a momentary bout
of disorientation. This is far better than the spit-takes I half

expected to occur when they learned that a critic was in the cast.

A stealth Silvia Cooper approaches me from behind and startles me. Dark-haired, crazy-eyed, and wearing a black button-down shirt and a pair of black skinny jeans seemingly spray-painted onto her legs, she looks like a goth Lady Macbeth. She offers me a firm handshake and stares me down during our brief and overly courteous conversation. "Looking forward to working with you," she says, but I know she is thinking, "Is this a dagger which I see before me?"

Thin skin.

As she spins on her stiletto heels to leave, tiny and adorable Erin Andrews takes her place. She is a blond pixie out of *A Midsummer Night's Dream*, who prances rather than walks as if always on the verge of taking flight. She gives me a tight, prolonged hug.

Short memory.

Brandon Steele—the young fellow playing Orlando, who shares the stage with Adam in every one of his scenes— seems to be avoiding me. His prominent head, with chiseled leading man features, can be seen working the room but never in my direction. I'm not sure why, since my reviews of his performances in this season's North Coast productions of *Love's Labour's Lost* and *Murder on the Nile* were very favorable. I've got to imagine that just having a critic in the inner circle of a meet-and-greet is pretty unnerving, which may also explain why the stage manager has yet to make eye contact with me as she mingles with everyone else.

It is not until Andrew Ganz does official cast member introductions and mentions my early Broadway credentials that everyone exhales and starts treating me a little more like a colleague and a little less like an unwelcome outsider. And when he shares the "What the fuck?!" audition story, and that expression quickly becomes a running joke among the cast and crew, I am pretty much accepted into the fold though I am still an unproven entity. By then, Brandon has worked his way toward me, puts a hand on my shoulder to say hello, and stands protectively to my left—like the Orlando he will be—for the rest of the meet-and-greet.

Director Michael Price steps forward. He moves with the grace and self-assuredness of a seasoned thespian and looks boyish for a fellow whose first professional directing job was thirty years ago. "The play," he says in a charming Irish accent that I did not expect and that makes everything he says sound downright playful, "sets its gaze on the virtue of redemption, does gymnastics with gender roles, sashays with sexual ambivalence, and celebrates the threshold of a new era of individuality."

A chorus of good-natured and well-timed "What the fucks?!" can be heard throughout the room, coming mostly from Michael's own design staff.

"There is no shortage of theater traditionalists," he continues, "who think that the works of Shakespeare need protection, rather than reinvention, as if their playhouses were museums, rather than places to play. But without a little literary blasphemy that transports an Elizabethan masterwork to a different time and temperament, how can those who don't look like the writer of the canon find a voice in it? And without a little artistic alchemy, how can outmoded themes and antiquated forms of expression be rendered more relevant?"

He goes on to mention a few of the artistically bold choices that have recently taken place in the Bard's own backyard. There was a gender-fluid production of *Romeo and Juliet* at the Royal Shakespeare Company, an all-female version of *Julius Caesar* set in a contemporary women's prison at the Donmar Warehouse, and an actor born with thalidomide-induced phocomelia cast to play the "deformed King" in Hull Truck Theatre's *Richard III.*

"So," he asks though he and his designers already know the answer, "what have we done with our production? We have taken it from 1620s England into the 1870s American West. In this rendition of Shakespeare's world, Duke Frederick's court is a decadent boom town populated with dance hall girls, backroom gamblers, opportunistic fur traders and loggers, and greedy fast-talking city slickers. Once the exiled Duke Senior—a would-be Henry David Thoreau—and his men escape into the utopian Forest of Arden, in the foothills of the central Rocky Mountains, they become a new breed of Americans who forge a new worldview and sense of equality. The intelligent and ever-resourceful Rosalind becomes a kind of metaphor for modern American womanhood. And the melancholy and cynical Jaques, who is one of Duke Senior's noblemen and delivers Shakespeare's famous 'All the World's a Stage' speech, has been cast as a woman to emphasize this play's focus on disconnected people searching for a place of belonging and to regain a lost sense of self."

Michael pauses for dramatic effect. He concludes with "Let all this inform what you bring to rehearsal tomorrow. And tomorrow. And tomorrow," which his brogue turns into a delightfully musical "tamarra."

OK, then.

Armed with ten lines in four scenes, I need to figure out how poor old Adam is pivotal in the virtuous establishment of redemption, in gender role gymnastics, and in the celebration of individuality in the Wild West. I've got some work to do.

Let the sexually ambivalent sashaying begin!

CHAPTER 17

Write on Cue

Memory, the warder of the brain.

Macbeth (Act I, Scene VII)

SASHAYING WILL HAVE to wait.

And forget about figuring out how Adam is pivotal in the virtuous establishment of redemption, in gender role gymnastics, and in the celebration of individuality. I'm having all sorts of trouble just memorizing his lines.

We're midway through the first week of rehearsals and all of the supporting actors arrived off book, most of the leading actors with volumes of dialogue are getting close, and I am still dependent on my script like an amateur. Worse, I can see Orlando mouthing my lines if there is a delay in me finding them on the page or getting them out of my mouth. I feel as if I am a more obvious fraud than George Plimpton was with the number "o" on his jersey, his New England accent in the huddle, and his ineptitude on the playing field. I half expect the director to yell "Kaufman, you've got your head up your ass" like my Pop Warner football coach used to.

At home, my teenage daughter Zoey runs lines with me at

the breakfast table and when she is through with her home-work in the evenings. At the gym in the morning, I do laps in the indoor pool with a copy of the script at each end of my lane and repeat lines in my head to the rhythm of my heartbeat. I drive to rehearsals listening to a self-recording of each line and attempt to recite them back. These are all the tricks of the trade I employed earlier in my acting career, but none seem to be working here. I tell myself I am just getting older, but I know it's Shakespeare.

So under the pretense of doing research for a behind-the-scenes article I am writing, I ask the production's veteran dramaturg, Anita Sanchez, if I can interview her for a piece about how actors during Shakespeare's day learned their lines. She's a historian by training and her job here is to help keep the production in the turn of the 20th century without losing sight of the Elizabethan context of the script. Too smart to be fooled by my pretense but too nice to turn me down, we chat over morning coffee.

She tells me that there was probably only one copy of the plays hand-penned by Shakespeare, which would be handed over to the lead actor of the production, who would write out his lines and the three or four cue lines that other characters would speak before his. He would then pass the manuscript on to the next featured actor, who passed it to the next, and so on until it was in the hands of the equivalent of the third murderer. "It would be a waste of paper, ink, and time to write out copies of the whole play," she says, "since actors only needed to memorize their own character's parts."

The eventual publishing of the plays, she tells me, was most likely reliant on pieced-together actors' cue scrolls that survived the production. The original manuscripts were probably in shambles by the time the plays opened, and the plays weren't published until seven years after Shakespeare's death.

"The act of transcribing their lines," she continues, "was a terrific memory aid, particularly since the actors had very limited time for rehearsal before the play would be up and running and there was very little time between plays being performed." I write all this down to keep up the illusion of an article but stop when Anita smiles every time I put pen to paper.

"Combine transcription with the education system of the time—where anybody who had been taught to read and write at a very early age was taught to memorize great chunks of text by rote—and actors could learn their lines in no time. Same thing with their stage direction."

I tell her that Shakespeare didn't seem to be a fan of stage direction. I've noticed only reference to actors entering and exiting in the script. "So Shakespeare was really, really clever as a writer/director—though we really don't know if a director was a thing back in the 16th century—because he knew that he wouldn't have time to waste trying to organize the actors before moving on to his next project. So what he did was introduce lots of instruction within the text itself."

Anita takes the *As You Like It* script from my hands and opens it to the first page of dialogue. "Look at your first line: 'Yonder comes my master, your brother.' That's a stage direction to enter for the actor playing Oliver. Then Orlando says: 'Go apart, Adam, and thou shalt hear how he will shake me up.' That's a stage direction for you."

After rehearsal, I go home and spend the night writing out one of Adam's lines and the line immediately before it, and do so over and over until they become familiar, retained, and then memorized. I do the same with all his other lines as well. It's 3 a.m. by the time I go to bed and the last thought I remember thinking as my head hit the pillow is whether I will still remember these lines when I wake up.

At breakfast, I ask Zoey to read my cues out loud, which she does with remarkable clarity—the fearing Shakespeare gene must skip a generation—and I recite my lines. They come out without expression but also without too many errors. We stare at each other in amazement. On the way out the door she suggests that I try this transcription thing with the dates of her birthday and my wedding anniversary. Couldn't hurt.

At rehearsal, I step into the performance space without a script and without quite knowing what to do with my hands. Brandon notices and, as Orlando, begins his opening line with some trepidation. As I await the cue to deliver my first line, I notice that other actors in the rehearsal room have stopped what they were doing to watch. So does the crew. And I see the director, Michael, inching closer to the taped boundary of the stage as either a show of moral support or to prepare himself to jump in and rescue me should Brandon attack in frustration if I drop a line. Actors can be temperamental.

When he completes his line, which is lengthy and full of exposition and Orlando backstory, Brandon steels himself for what is about to come, expecting the worst by the look of him. I manage to nail all three of Adam's brief spurts of dialogue in Act I, Scene I, and stumble through with moderate success his Act II, Scene III diatribes. I execute with precision and proper emotion his one line while dying in Act II, Scene VI and, after being carried onto the stage and into good Duke Senior's camp by Orlando in Act II, Scene VII, do the same with Adam's short and reedy near-death expression of thanks. I am soaked in sweat by the time Duke Senior says to me, "Good old man, thou art right welcome as thy master" and everyone exits.

There's high fives and "Huzzahs" from everyone in the rehearsal room. Except for the stage manager, who yells, "Back in ten" to announce a short break and does so without fanfare and still without eye contact.

CHAPTER 18

Killing Off Adam

Out, out, brief candle! Life's but a walking
shadow, a poor player that struts and frets his
hour upon the stage and then is heard no more.

Macbeth (Act V, Scene V)

I'VE GOT NOTHING but time on my hands this week, what
with Adam not factoring into the Act III scenes currently
being blocked and rehearsed. In fact, Adam no longer makes
an appearance in this play.

I'm at rehearsal, taking notes in my capacity as a clandestine critic. I've already written behind-the-scenes articles about how, at the first table reading, the play came to
life as actors started to find a voice for their characters. I've
described how these superb actors add texture and tempo
and build layers of complexity at each rehearsal, and how
this has encouraged me to work on old man attributes that
add authenticity to Adam's short time on stage. I've doc-
umented the actors' backstage rituals, superstitions, and
prerehearsal warm-ups. I've even written a piece about how
actors during Shakespeare's day learned their lines, just to
save face with the dramaturg.

A week ago I would have been grateful for my character's quick exit from the stage and this opportunity to relax, observe, and learn. But now the more confident reawakened actor in me wants to be on stage and I am curious as to why Shakespeare made Adam dead.

In Arden in Act II, Adam nearly dies of exhaustion and hunger during his final scene. His master, Orlando, tells Duke Senior, "there is an old poor man/Who after me hath many a weary step/Limped in pure love" and then old, poor, limping Adam is heard from no more. But his death is never actually seen or discussed.

The old guy has been nothing if not a loyal and beloved family servant, lending Orlando an ear when his master complains about his sorrows, offering a warning when Orlando's angry brother approaches and when his house is set on fire in a murderous plot, and he gives Orlando his life's savings so the two of them can escape to the forest. And yet he doesn't show up at his master's marriage in the play's final scene. Surely he must be dead. But the evidence is merely circumstantial.

I decide to take this up with the director during lunch break.

I explain to the stage manager, who orchestrates such meetings, that whether or not Adam dies informs how I play him while alive. "About 155 of Shakespeare's characters die in his plays. More than half die offstage and many—like Adam—do so without a witness," I tell her, realizing with each word just how ridiculous I must sound. She just looks at me without response or expression, which is a marked improvement over her earlier avoidance, and schedules an appointment.

Michael had announced at the meet-and-greet that he has an open-door policy, but it quickly became clear that he never meant to enforce it and never expected anyone to follow up on it. Still, he's pleased to see me when I arrive at his small office down the hallway from the rehearsal space. Thick skin.

"Adam is simply too old to help initiate the new social order that takes place during this play," Michael says as he closes his door so we can chat in private. "Perhaps Shakespeare didn't want some old man and all that he represents standing around on stage as the younger generation is taking charge. He is given no more lines, he has no more entrance cues, and no more words about him are spoken by any of the other characters. Not even Orlando speaks his name. And what," he asks, already knowing the answer, "is Adam's final line in his final scene?"

"'Dear Master, I can't go any farther,'" I recite. "'Here lie I down and measure out my grave. Farewell, kind master.'"

"'Lie I down. My grave. Farewell.' Yeah, Asher, Adam's pretty damn well dead," says Michael.

"But," I counter, "in that same scene Orlando encourages Adam to live. He says, 'Why, how now, Adam? No greater heart in thee? Live a little, comfort a little, cheer thyself a little. Thy conceit is nearer death than thy powers.' So maybe Adam lives, for no other reason than to be the loyal and beloved servant that he is and do what his master requests: live a little."

"Plus," I add before Michael can get a word in edgewise, "the Forest of Arden is a magical place. It represents escape, while Duke Frederick's court represents corruption. The forest has the power to convert the evil Duke into a caring brother toward the end of the play. Orlando and his hate-filled brother Oliver reconcile. And everyone falls in love and gets married."

There's a pause.

"Adam should make an appearance at the wedding," I declare with the same level of surprise in my voice that I see on Michael's face. "He's been rejuvenated by the power of the forest, the power of love, and the power of the new world order being created by Rosalind and Orlando. Adam should be at their wedding."

"But Shakespeare didn't put him in that scene," says Michael.

"Shakespeare didn't set the play in the Wild West in the 1800s," is my return volley.

I try unsuccessfully to read what Michael is thinking as he squints at me for a long, hard moment and rubs his forehead while doing so. My instinctive response is to squint back with even greater intensity.

"Hmmm, Adam not dead." He grabs a half-eaten sandwich that's been lying in wait on his desk and walks out the door. "We're back," announces the stage manager.

A week later, after walking through an initial run of the wedding scene and then setting up for a second runthrough, Michael stops what he is doing and yells, "Adam, get in there."

CHAPTER 19

Playbill

Let me be that I am and seek not to alter me.

Much Ado About Nothing (Act I, Scene III)

*T*ODAY I WROTE my playbill bio for the North Coast Theater production of *As You Like It*, which opens shortly.

My fifty-word blurb reads: "Asher Kaufman (*Adam*). North Coast Theater debut. I dedicate my performance to Keanu Reeves. His pouty Don John in the film *Much Ado About Nothing* offers hope to all the rest of us performing Shakespeare with no particular aptitude for this art."

CHAPTER 20

Suppressing Shakespeare

*By my soul I swear, there is no power
in the tongue of man to alter me.*

The Merchant of Venice (Act IV, Scene I)

*R*EHEARSALS HAVE KEPT me out of the office and limited my writing to the behind-the-scenes pieces that are starting to appear in print and online. So my editor Mark has been forwarding me ideas for some opinion pieces he would also like me to write to earn my keep at the *Chronicle*. The one about Shakespeare and Jews captures my attention.

The inspiration for this idea was former Vice President Joe Biden. Not long ago, he referred to those who make bad loans as "Shylocks." He was speaking on the occasion of the 40th anniversary of the Legal Services Corporation, a nonprofit that helps fund legal aid. After being called out by the Anti-Defamation League, Biden apologized for his "poor choice of words."

The word "Shylock" is an eponym derived from the Jewish character in Shakespeare's *The Merchant of Venice*, who demanded a pound of flesh from the torso of the merchant Antonio as an overdue loan repayment. Shylock's greed, Machiavellian ways, and Jewish identity have become indelibly linked for over 400 years. He's not just a Jew; he's "The Jew."

In fact, throughout *The Merchant of Venice*, good Christians depersonalize and alienate Shylock by refusing to use his given name. Instead, they call him "the villain Jew," "the currish Jew," and "the devil in the likeness of the Jew."

They also undermine his faith. After Shylock quotes the Bible to make a point, Antonio tells a friend: "The devil can cite Scripture for his purpose. An evil soul producing holy witness is like a villain with a smiling cheek, a goodly apple rotten at the heart. O, what a goodly outside falsehood hath!" At the end of the play, Shylock is offered an insulting alternative to being put to death: become a Christian.

Jews were regularly villainized in Elizabethan plays, the result of centuries of bigotry, massacre, forced conversion, and expulsion throughout Europe. In fact, three centuries before *The Merchant of Venice* was written, England became the first country in medieval Europe to expel its Jewish population. Christopher Marlowe's *The Jew of Malta*, which was written nearly a decade before *The Merchant of Venice*, features a particularly monstrous Jew who sums up his code of conduct by stating: "First, be thou void of these affections: Compassion, love, vain hope, and heartless fear; be moved at nothing; see thou pity none." A charmer. Ben Jonson does the same in *The Alchemist*, written nearly a decade after *The Merchant of Venice*.

It is very likely that neither Shakespeare, Marlowe, nor Jonson ever actually met a Jew.

In the article Mark wants me to write, I am to ask whether the Protestant Shakespeare's anti-Semitism should be censored and to offer an opinion on the subject.

He emails me a press release that crossed his desk, sent

out by the Oregon Shakespeare Festival. The company had just commissioned translations of all thirty-nine of Shakespeare's plays into contemporary English, so that they will be more accessible to today's audiences. Thirty-six playwrights paired with dramaturgs were being assigned to the task. And by commissioning a diverse group of playwrights—more than half would be women and more than half would be writers of color—the OSF hoped to bring fresh voices and perspectives to Shakespeare's work.

While the task of the OSF team was to translate only those lines that interfered with contemporary comprehension, perhaps, Mark suggests, it could also translate lines that interfered with contemporary compassion.

"What if, in *The Merchant of Venice*, every reference to Shylock as the evil personification of what was deemed a repugnant religion was substituted with his given name to humanize him?" I write. "What if every anti-Semitic utterance was tweaked, toned down, or deleted? Would this be a disservice to Shakespeare's works, and would it impact on the rampant anti-Semitism that exists beyond the pages and in our own time?"

For the article, I interviewed James S. Shapiro, a Columbia University Professor of English and Comparative Literature, who has given serious consideration to the notion of censoring Shakespeare in general and *The Merchant of Venice* in particular.

"To avert our gaze from what the play reveals about the relationship between cultural myths and people's identities will not make irrational and exclusionary attitudes disappear," he argued.

"These darker impulses remain so elusive, so hard to identify in the normal course of things, that only in instances like productions of this play do we get to glimpse these cultural fault lines. Censoring the play," warned Shapiro, "is always more dangerous than staging it."

To my surprise, I find myself agreeing with him. I write, "We stand to lose much more by translating and simplifying Shakespeare than we stand to gain. Maybe it's the hard and the hard-to-take in these plays that makes the work great." This from the guy who not long ago was clutching onto volumes of No Fear Shakespeare for dear life, having fever dreams about the complexities of Shakespeare-speak, and begging a dramaturg for assistance. But now I recommend that we leave the work alone.

I even suggest in the article that, maybe, Shakespeare was purposefully recording the views of his time for posterity; that *The Merchant of Venice* was intended to call out anti-Semitism rather than promote it.

"In matters of suppression or censorship," I write, "to be or not to be should never be the question."

CHAPTER 21

A Sense of Foreboding

I am surprised with an uncouth fear; a chilling
sweat o'er-runs my trembling joints: My heart
suspects more than mine eye can see.

Titus Andronicus (Act II, Scene III)

SOMEONE IN THE cast is messing with me.

Rehearsals have moved to the Hedley Theatre as the production heads into tech week, preview performances, and then our opening night and, for the past few days, I have found a small white envelope on my dressing room chair. In it is an unsigned, typewritten quote from a Shakespeare play that offers some form of intimidation. Shakespeare's plays are full of foreboding—vague but suggestive and intimidating references intended to prepare a character and the audience for the drama or tragedy to come—and someone has thought to aim them at me.

Yesterday, I found this quote from *Twelfth Night*: "If this were played upon a stage now, I could condemn it as an improbable fiction." Someone thinks my performance is not up to par.

Today was a quote from *Julius Caesar*: "Are not you moved,

when all the sway of earth shakes like a thing unfirm?" Not only is my performance inadequate; someone thinks it is undermining the integrity of the entire production.

This is personal and, quite frankly, quite effective. No amount of hard work, therapy, or Magic 8 Ball prognostication can completely undo the fear of all things Shakespeare that has amassed over the years. I have memorized the lines, but I am still struggling with matching the fluid, natural presentation of the other performers. I'm nervous about opening night. I'm worried about what the critics will think. And these notes out of nowhere don't help.

Who would do such a thing, and why?

It is obviously someone who knows his or her way around Shakespeare's works, which points an accusatory finger at everyone, but particularly the ten classically trained actors who are members of the North Coast Theater company. And since the notes are always waiting for me after I've completed my scenes in the first two acts of the play, that someone is not one of the actors playing Orlando, his brother Oliver, the melancholic nobleman Jaques, Duke Senior, or the Duke's two attendants, who all share the stage with me.

Of those still in contention, it is most likely someone who has received a negative review in the *Cleveland Jewish Chronicle* and takes it seriously enough to want to retaliate.

Thin-skinned Silvia Cooper aka Rosalind aka Lady Macbeth aka Gertrude McFuzz comes to mind.

I should just ignore these notes, which are unprofessional and inappropriate. Wasn't it Hamlet who asked whether 'tis nobler in the mind to suffer the slings and arrows of outrageous fortune? And he knew a thing or two about intimidation. But I do admire the craft behind these notes. And I am terribly tempted to follow Hamlet's lead by taking arms against a sea of troubles, and by opposing end them. Which I do.

But instead of words of intimidation I offer insults, since there is no shortage of really great Elizabethan barbs in the Bard's plays. And to show Silvia that anonymity is childish, I sign each handwritten note before placing it on her chair and scampering away from her dressing room like a five-year-old prank-ringing a neighbor's doorbell.

"Away, you starvelling, you elf-skin, you dried neat's-tongue, bull's-pizzle, you stock-fish!" (*Henry IV, Part I*)

"I must tell you friendly in your ear, sell when you can, you are not for all markets." (*As You Like It*)

"You are as a candle, the better part burnt out." (*Henry IV, Part II*)

I have other notes at the ready—something clever about a "scurvy companion," a "canker-blossom" and one about a "stewed prune"—but as I am about to enter Silvia's back-stage dressing room to deliver today's installment I see her through the open door getting ready for post-lunch rehearsal. And she sees me. She jumps out of her chair and quickly approaches me in the hallway. She stops just inches from my face and plants a big kiss on my lips.

"Asher, you dear man," she says while holding me in her arms. "I've been so nervous about doing this play, playing this role. How did you know? Your fun notes have been keeping me from taking myself too seriously and are a great kindness. What a thoughtful thing." And she kisses me again.

That night I get a call from my friend Larry, who asks how rehearsals are going, whether it would put too much pressure on me if he attended opening night, and whether I could get him some comps. "And how have the notes been working out?"

There's a pause on my part. A long one. "Those are from you?"

"Of course. Little pieces of encouragement. Quotes from someone in a Shakespeare play who is so worse off than you. I thought you would find them comforting."

I am both relieved and peeved. "How'd they make their way into my dressing room?"

"A member of the crew is a patient. I still have your copies of No Fear Shakespeare, by the way."

"The notes weren't signed."

"Why would they be? Who else would do such a thing? And you're welcome."

CHAPTER 22

Some Quality Time

There is flattery in friendship.

Henry V (Act III, Scene VII)

*M*Y BEHIND-THE-SCENES ARTICLES are starting to gain some traction among my readers and now everyone in the show has a fascinating story they believe should be shared in the *Chronicle*.

It wasn't that long ago when, at the meet-and-greet, everyone I encountered appeared genuinely disinterested when I introduced myself. Now I am being trailed by classically trained actors who, like lost newborn fawns, are attempting to cross-species imprint with a critic. Some of the more veteran performers just happen to be hanging out at my usual off-stage haunts with an epic tale to tell.

In the restroom earlier today, two chatty actors saddled up to the urinals on each side of mine with such precision and nonchalance that it could have been choreographed by Twyla Tharp. As I have done at so many intermissions at so many opening night productions I've reviewed, I found myself feigning a preoccupation with peeing—as if I just discovered something fascinating and new—in order to avoid conversation. And because I had to linger significantly in order to outlast these rather impressive and patient urinators, I got back to rehearsal a tad late. "Sorry, I was method-acting old Adam's incontinence during a bathroom break," I said to Michael on my way to the stage.

Every encounter with an actor about a possible article calls attention to the fact that I am still more outcast than cast member, so I decide to put an end to it in one fell swoop by posting a note on the backstage bulletin board where the actors sign in each day. It asks anyone with a story for the *Chronicle* to meet me for drinks at the burger-and-beer place across the street from our building. I write that "while I can't promise that everyone's tale will make it into the paper, the drinks are on Old Adam."

Actors are infamous for loving to tell stories about themselves. But they love free food and liquor even more, so nearly everyone in the cast is in attendance. Some crew members show up as well, as does our dramaturg. But not the stage manager, whose name I have learned is Kate.

After a few rounds and increasingly loud and lively conversation, I tap my beer bottle with a fork to get everyone's attention so I can announce that we should start the storytelling. "Make sure you have a drink," I tell them, "but keep in mind that poor Old Adam gave all of his money to Orlando to subsidize their trip to Arden and he is living on a very small pension. Plus his meager monthly annuity payouts."

Frank, who plays Orlando's abusive and condescending older brother, is the first to stand up and speak. He mentions the irony of earning his Master of Fine Arts at Kent State University, moving to New York City to make it on Broadway, and now finding himself working back in Ohio. In the five years he's lived in Brooklyn, he says, every job has been out of town at regional theaters. He's never worked in New York and never lived in his apartment for more than a week or two at a time. He gets a few "amens" from those living a similar lifestyle. "By the way," he adds before taking his seat, "I wasn't able to sublet my place before coming here, and then our show heads off to Taos, and my next gig is with the Idaho Shakespeare Festival in Boise. So if anyone knows anyone who is working in NYC but is from out of town and needs a place to rent and doesn't mind two roommates and a few cats, let me know."

A young attendant to Duke Frederick, I believe his name is Peter, is next up. He proudly announces that his agent just booked him a television gig that he hopes will be his big break and "launch a career in small-screen storytelling." He landed a one-and-done speaking role in an episode of the long-running crime drama *Law & Order: Special Victims Unit.* A cry of "Dun, dun"—the show's stylized and overly dramatic sound of a jail cell locking—fills the room. And everyone but Peter laughs because they know the TV show has become a common and very short-term day job for stage actors who, afterward, are still stage actors. Deflated, Peter slowly takes his seat and orders another drink.

Phoebe, who plays a nameless dance hall girl early in the play and a nameless shepherdess later on, offers Peter her gin and tonic until his own arrives. And Charlie, who plays both Duke Frederick and Duke Senior in our production, comes to the rescue by admitting that his audition reel includes clips from an episode of the police procedural *NCIS,* where he played the dead guy, and a daytime soap opera, all of which helped pay the rent and land him his current job as a nine-year member of the North Coast Theater. He kindly omits having also been in a national commercial for

Mastercard and playing a supporting role in most of season six of *Grey's Anatomy*.

Dani, who plays a young country girl named Audrey, talks about her recent experience acting in "Homegrown Christmas," "Tingle Around the Clock," and "Mingle All the Way," which were three of the thirty-seven original and low-budget yuletide tales that the Hallmark Channel ran from October to December as part of its "Countdown to Christmas" made-for-TV movie lineup. She shares the inanity that is wearing layers of winter clothes and "acting all Christmassy" during a summer shoot. And she explains the challenge of playing the same type of best-friend character in three nearly identical stories that featured attractive but forgotten 1990s TV actors as the romantically involved but mismatched couple. "And I'm still finding holiday glitter in my panties."

They talk about the shows that made them eligible for Actors' Equity membership and the pros and cons of going on national tours. They talk about the career paths they sidestepped that their parents would have preferred. When the discussion turns to the worst reviews ever received, Erin mentions how she was delegated to the Seventh Circle of hell in the *Cleveland Jewish Chronicle* for her performance in *Legends!*

All eyes turn toward me, but instead of the conversation going south, I am asked to tell one or two of my own stories from the stage. After I recount my high school experience with *Macbeth*, my colleagues start buying me drinks. And when the topic turns to oddest audition choices, I share how, for my audition for the Broadway revival of *Fiddler,* I wore a fake pair of long Hasidic sidelocks sewed onto a knitted yarmulke with the New York Yankees insignia that I had picked up on a whim at a novelty store in Times Square. I looked like I had just walked over from the Brooklyn neighborhood of Crown Heights, rather than lived in the underfed, over-worked, turn-of-the-20th-century village of Anatevka.

When Sharon—the show's melancholic Jaques—starts doing tequila shots with the actor who plays a country vicar and two guys she picked up at the bar, I decide that it is time to go home. And so I pick up the check and bid everyone goodnight.

I don't know if you can put a price on what it feels like to be finally accepted as an insider, but $253.75 plus tip seems like a good deal.

CHAPTER 23

Lenny in the First Row

If by chance I talk a little wild,
forgive me; I had it from my father.

Henry VIII (Act I, Scene IV)

*W*E HAVE BEGUN a week of preview performances of *As You Like It* and for the first one, a matinee, the North Coast Theater powers-that-be decide to pad the house with an audience bused in from surrounding nursing homes and senior citizen community centers. A full Hedley Theatre helps the director monitor reactions and make necessary adjustments in the production. It also allows the actors to refine their comic timing.

There's Lenny in the first row, surrounded by dozens of his fellow assisted living facility residents.

When most theatergoers take their seats, lost in the anticipation of an evening of live entertainment, so much around them goes unnoticed or underappreciated. The ornamental rosettes, acanthus leaves, and assorted curlicues that decorate crown molding. The meticulous notes from the dramaturg buried in the middle of the playbill. Eighty-eight-year-old Lenny—the patron saint of local theater and my dad—in the first row.

To say that he loves theater is an understatement. It is his primary passion and his most fulfilling pleasure. It does not define him, but theater most certainly completes him. He is an adoring admirer and voracious promoter with equal appreciation for Equity performers and earnest amateurs. He is unabashedly open to theater in all its many manifestations and greets every production as if it were his first and has the potential to be his last.

Lenny is an innocent and a kid in a candy store. He is astoundingly unaware or unconcerned that he is the only man buying a ticket for the national tour of *Menopause: The Musical*, one of the few straight men in the audience of an all-gay revue at convergence-continuum, and the only octogenarian sitting through a production at Talespinner Children's Theatre without a child in tow. Lenny is a Caucasian Jew at Karamu House, the oldest African American theater in the United States, during a production of *Black Nativity*.

There he is in the first row.

A Beachwood, Ohio, resident, he grew up in the melting pot of New York City during the 1930s and 1940s surrounded by vaudeville houses off Time Square, Yiddish theater on the lower east side, small-scale "Straw Hat" circuit productions on Long Island and upstate, and grand Broadway shows that showcased the likes of Lunt and Fontanne, Ethel Merman, and Mary Martin.

With a little prodding, Lenny will recall sixty-year-old performances as if they were yesterday and recount yesterday's performance with specificity and perspective. With no prodding whatsoever, he is happy to share his perspective with the stranger in the seat next to him or the usher who showed him the seat. During an interview I did with actor Joel Grey to promote an appearance he was making at Playhouse Square, I mentioned that my dad and I took in a midnight one-man show he performed in the Grand Ballroom of New York's Waldorf Astoria thirty years ago. The then-eighty-four-year-old actor was able to recall more details about what he performed in the show than me. My dad, when asked, was able to recall more details than Joel Grey.

We are running today's show with all the production elements that have been built to date but, typical of preview performances, some are just now being introduced and others are still works in progress. Pieces and parts of costuming, including Adam's boots, are still in transit.

When some light cues are mishandled and set pieces are askew on stage during today's performance, they seem to warrant a reaction by the senior theatergoers in the audience in the form of a call-and-response led by Lenny in the first row. "Well, there's a late entrance," says my dad for all to hear. "My, my, my," reply his cronies. They don't miss a thing. And my dad applauds each of my entrances and exits.

All this is a test of the cast's discipline, which we fail. It is impossible not to break character and smile with each whistle from a maladjusted hearing aid or at the sound of our own voices delayed by one to three seconds by the in-house headphones worn by most of the elderly in attendance and turned up to the maximum setting. And it is hard not to laugh when we hear two women with their headphones blaring, arguing loudly about why Ganymede, who is Rosalind dressed as a boy, is in love with Orlando.

"It's not natural, boys liking boys," yells one woman to the woman in the next seat, oblivious to her volume.

"It's Shakespeare," yells the other even louder. "That's what they did back then."

During intermission, the cast has plenty to talk about.

When I mention that my dad is the ringleader of all the play-by-play patrons, everyone breaks protocol and immediately heads into the house to say hello and give him a hug. The show is delayed by fifteen minutes because my dad has to introduce each cast member to his buddies, saving the show's leading lady Rosalind—who had kissed him on the forehead—for last.

When the play continues, Lenny and his gang are no less vocal. I've got to imagine that this is what it was like for actors during Shakespeare's day, when a sea of groundlings stood at the foot of the stage cheering, taunting, and throwing fruit.

During bows I look out into the audience to make eye contact with my dad who, at intermission, seemed prouder seeing me in this show than he ever was sitting next to me while I was reviewing a show. There's Lenny, fast asleep in the first row.

CHAPTER 24

Reflections of Opening Night

The very substance of the ambitious
is merely the shadow of a dream.

Hamlet (Act II, Scene II)

I'M DRIVING DOWNTOWN to the sold-out opening night
performance of the show and I do not run into a sea of
pedestrians dressed to the nines in furs and pearls, tuxes and
ties, trying to cross the street and head toward the Hedley
Theatre.

I glance at the theater's marquee and it looks as if I am
still appearing in *As You Like It* and not *Troilus and Cressida*.

When I get to the stage door, I'm confronted by the
security guard, actually stewed to the gills and practically
falling off his too-small stool, but he is not reciting Shakespeare. Once inside the theater, I run into Andrew Ganz,
who tells me to "break a leg" and he is not wearing pumpkin
pants or pointy shoes. I am not naked. There is no Orson
Welles in the wings. What hump?

Good to go.

One hour before curtain, before our audience arrives,
most actors are busy backstage eating snacks and checking
props while others take to the stage to stretch their bodies

and warm up their vocal cords in preparation for their performances. The assorted guttural squawks, nasal honks, and
shrill vocalizations sound like an episode of *Animals Gone
Wild* on PBS. My pre-show preparation entails pacing and
pondering fleeting moments of self-doubt.

On my dressing room chair is an unsigned note with
a quote from *Julius Caesar* that reads: "Cowards die many
times before their deaths; the valiant never taste of death
but once." Thanks for the encouragement, Larry. Very reas-
suring.

One half-hour before curtain, several partially costumed
actors visit dressing rooms to administer hugs and heart-
felt sentiments about working together on this production.
Brandon Steele, who overheard my high school *Macbeth*
story at the burger-and-beer joint the other night, comes
into the dressing room and places some stage putty in my
makeup kit, which I find hilarious. Kate, the stage manager,
circulates backstage and gives handwritten last-minute director's notes to actors. Mine reads: "Join in on the dancing in
the wedding scene rather than just observe. Fortunately, no
disco!" Thick skin and good memory.

At 7:25 p.m., the cast of sixteen forms a circle on the stage
behind the closed curtain, holds hands, and offers up some
positive thoughts for Charlie, who plays Duke Frederick
and Duke Senior. He received some unfortunate, but not
unexpected news from his doctor earlier today. He gets a
kiss from everyone before we silently disperse to take our
places.

It is amazing, really, how this odd assortment of artists
has become a family that is now intimately familiar with
each member's talents, comfortable with each other's creative choices, and concerned about each other's well-being.

There is a bold, even brazen confidence among these players as they prepare to set out onto the ice, where anything unexpected can and most likely will happen. Me, I've already sweated through my costume.

On the other side of the curtain, Andrew Ganz bounds down the house-left aisle and up onto the stage to do his opening night introduction of board members in attendance and sponsors for the season. "Turn your cell phones off," he says, "and unwrap your candy at this time. Sit back and enjoy the comedy *As You Like It*."

I am calmed by the pre-show tranquility of my fellow performers and the amount of preparation, on stage and off, that led to this evening. I take a deep breath as the lights come up and the curtain rises, hear neither cicadas nor the high-pitched staccato of a little girl's whimper, and walk onto the stage two steps behind Orlando to start the show and—miracle of miracles—speak some Shakespeare.

The stage is a wonderland, courtesy of scenic design that blends stark realism with heightened fantasy. Toward the back, around the perimeter of the wood panel flooring, are dozens of thick tree trunks that reach up to the ceiling with a thick green forest behind them. At center stage in the background hangs a large-scale painting depicting a lively bordello scene in an elaborate gold frame that establishes the setting of Duke Frederick's court, represented by a decadent boom town. The bordello painting gets swapped out for a landscape featuring hills shrouded in haze in a primitive wood frame when the setting becomes the utopian Forest of Arden in the foothills of the central Rocky Mountains.

I forgot how alive I feel being on a professional stage in front of a sold-out crowd. In my capacity as a critic, sitting in the audience for an opening night production is always exciting and certainly triggers memories of performing, which no doubt inspire that occasional itch to perform again. But standing on the Hedley Theatre stage, lost in the world of this play while simultaneously monitoring and assessing all the many moving pieces and parts taking place around me and beyond the audience's view, is thrilling.

And, truth be told, having the opportunity to speak words that were first spoken on a stage over 400 years ago and to speak them well—to wade in the waters of the picturesque beachfront property of Illyria—adds a little something to the experience.

The rest is silence and a bit of a blur. Muscle memory kicks in and all my character's lines, reactions, and movements come out as planned. I'm aware that the audience—which includes Patty and the kids, Larry and a date, and a few other friends, acquaintances, and work colleagues—reacts in all the right ways and does so at all the right places. I'm aware that everyone's performance seems energized by the pomp of opening night and the full house. I'm aware of how often my fellow actors squeeze my arm as a sign of support and approval while we stand offstage and await our next entrance.

After my scenes are over, I retreat backstage to the common area Green Room to relax and wait for intermission, during which actors check their phones, refuel, and rehydrate before returning to the stage. When the play begins again, I fetch my pen and pad from my dressing room and head for the stage to stand in the darkness of the wings and away from other actors' traffic patterns to watch the scenes that Adam is not in and make a few final observations for my last behind-the-scenes installment in the *Chronicle*.

I start to write about how the remarkable on-stage chemistry and physicality of Rosalind and Celia, who are cousins, best friends, and inseparable partners, are surely informed and enriched by Silvia and Erin's marriage and off-stage affection for one another. I start to write about Sharon's impressive transformation from rowdy, tequila-swilling bad-ass at the burger-and-beer joint to the tender-hearted, poetic traveler Jaques and how tonight's rendition of the "All the World's a Stage" speech is particularly melancholic due to the immense hangover she earned last night. I start to write about Charlie's ability to maintain Duke Senior's driving romanticism and glass-half-full philosophy despite receiving a medical diagnosis that would have buckled the knees of most of us.

And then I stop writing, realizing that I no longer have the same level of desired detachment that I had when I started out as an embedded journalist. I've lost my George Plimptonesque objectivity and grown way too close to these people. These final reflections are not for public consumption. Leaving my pad and pen on the prop table, I reenter the stage for the climactic wedding of Rosalind and Orlando, Celia and Oliver, the shepherd Silvius and shepherdess Phoebe, and the country girl Audrey and the fool Touchstone.

The ceremony transitions into a festive celebration where the director has swapped out Elizabethan tunes for lively country & western music played by an on-stage six-person string band. The ensemble breaks into a beautifully choreographed and wonderfully joyous line dance with moments of improvisation to keep things fun and not too obviously orchestrated. The trees in our Arden forest are strung with party lanterns, brightly colored flags, and coin-sized metallic discs meant to refract the light and add some sparkle. The scene is magical and unfolds as if in slow motion.

I stay in the background but, per my new marching orders, start stomping and clapping with the music and then grab onto a nearby ensemble member for an unrehearsed old Adam rendition of "Cotton Eye Joe." At about the time my thighs start to tighten from failing to properly stretch out before the show, abetted by the newly arrived boots I have yet to break in, Orlando grabs me for an impromptu two-step around the stage. This tweaks and then tears one hamstring and, when he spins me out to replace me with his newly-betrothed Rosalind, tears the other. Momentum carries me just out of harm's way from the dancing denizens of Arden, but not close enough to any viable exit to get off the stage.

So there I stand amid the giant trees in front of a sold-out audience, a grinning, weeping, and fairly immobile idiot during the dialogue and final dance that ends the show. Brandon, who had heard the pop of my hamstring during our dance, comes and fetches me for the curtain call. Old Adam's limp was never more pronounced nor more authentic than when I step forward—supported by Brandon on one side and a very concerned Silvia on the other—to take my excruciatingly painful bow as the curtain falls and opening night ends.

Back in my dressing room, I sit and wonder whether I am a good enough actor and Adam is a small enough part so that no one in the audience—particularly the critics in attendance—noticed my Peter O'Toole moment.

On my makeup table I find two bags of ice and two ibuprofen to ease the pain in the back of my thighs. Attached to one bag by a small piece of bright pink glow tape is a Xerox copy of an old review I wrote of a North Coast Theater production of *The Taming of the Shrew*.

CHAPTER 25

Come On and Kiss Me, Kate

I do desire we may be better strangers.

As You Like It (Act III, Scene II)

I MISSED YOU AT the restaurant the other night," I yell ahead to our stage manager, Kate, as we both walk down the now-dark and empty backstage hallway toward the theater's rear exit. We are the last to leave. I'm off to meet friends and family at a nearby restaurant for an opening night after-show celebration and post-mortem, and her plans are to disappear into the artificial light of the outdoor parking lot and head back to a tiny near-west-side apartment that is empty save for a dozen cats and some broken dreams. I'm just guessing that last part, since I know nothing about her whatsoever.

"Thanks for the ice. And what's with the newspaper clipping?"

She stops, turns, and speaks to me for the first time since the first day of rehearsal. "That's from a North Coast show I stage managed, and it was the only time my name appeared in a review," she said. "It was a great review and it made me happy, but the sign of good stage management is that no one notices the stage management."

"Yeah," I say, "but I'm trained to notice. And great stage

management deserves to be called out so that everyone can notice. I'd never seen a show that hit on all cylinders like that."

"Well . . ."

"So why did you leave me the review instead of coming by to chat? And why haven't we ever chatted? I thought you hated me."

"I wanted to let you know how thankful I was for the mention, but didn't want to cry in front of a cast member. I have to maintain my reputation as a stone-cold hard-ass."

"I'm assuming that's from the official Stage Management Handbook you guys get when you pass the course," I tease. "There's a course, right? And you passed, right?"

"More like a seminar. An online weekend workshop, really. It was pass/fail."

"Got any plans tonight? I'm meeting up with a few friends and family members and it would be great if you joined us. Plus, I think I need some help waddling out of here. The ice was great, but my legs are killing me."

Kate, who is shorter than I am, puts my arm around her shoulder and her arm around my waist. "I'm pretty sure the official Stage Management Handbook recommends a fireman's carry," she says as we slowly head toward the bluish light emanating from the cracks around the stage door, "but I am officially off duty and you are non-union."

"You know," I murmur as the ibuprofen and post-show euphoria start to kick in, "this is kind of like that 'this is the beginning of a beautiful friendship' final scene in *Casablanca,* if Bogie had blown out his hamstrings chasing after Ingrid Bergman. And, of course, if 'La Marseillaise' was playing in the background."

"That would make me the lovable authority figure,

Louis," Kate says as she kicks open the stage door and we head out into the misty night, "and I'm not sure I could live with that."

CHAPTER 26

The Reviews Are In

The play's the thing.

Hamlet (Act II, Scene II)

QUESTION: HOW MANY theater critics does it take to screw in a light bulb?

Answer: All of them. One to be highly critical of the design element, one to critique the performance of the bulb itself, and all to suggest that they could most certainly build a better light bulb.

While many theater critics believe that they can write a better play in their sleep than the ones they review for a living, very few have actually done so and fewer still—perhaps only *The Saturday Review's* George Bernard Shaw, *The New York Tribune's* George S. Kaufman, the *New Republic's* Eric Bentley, and the *Bristol Evening World's* Tom Stoppard—have turned it into a going concern.

I can't name another critic who is also a working actor.

There are good reasons. The most pragmatic is that performing on stage for consecutive weeks keeps the critic from reviewing others on stage for consecutive weeks, which is counterproductive professionally. Good thing I have an understanding editor who finds that my behind-the-scenes pieces are an interesting, albeit self-serving, replacement for a few reviews.

But the greatest disincentive for turning from critic to actor is that being on stage opens you up to unmitigated, unmerciful highly public scrutiny by colleagues who critique actors for a living and have made names for themselves by inflicting pain with creative prose. And a fellow critic who has the audacity to step across that imaginary line that separates "us" from "them" is just asking for an ass-kicking.

And so I ignore the reviews of *As You Like It* when they hit the newsstands and the Internet the morning after the opening night performance. But my editor Mark does not. He calls me at home to let me know that the show received unanimous raves and that I came out unscathed largely because I am unmentioned. "Not a word," says Mark, who interprets this as a slight, but I look at it as a great kindness and a huge relief that none of the reviews had anything to do with me or my minor character.

"Well, there was one," says Mark sheepishly.

In my absence, Mark asked eager intern Gwen to attend and review the opening night production of *As You Like It* for the *Chronicle*. "I wanted something in the paper that puts closure on your behind-the-scenes adventure," he tells me, "and she was more than happy to do it. She has a minor in theater management."

I hang up, go online, and find the article posted on the paper's website.

Gwen is a very good writer who has yet to find her voice in the limited number of articles with her byline that have made it into print. She found it here. It is very much grounded in the paper's core mission to view things through a Jewish lens and attempt to find a "Jewish angle" in every story which, for a sophomore from a private Jesuit university, must have been a bit of a stretch. And so she has placed me and my Jewishness awkwardly but earnestly front and center of her review.

She loves what North Coast Theater has done with the play and she loves the performances turned in by Silvia and Brandon. "Most performances of *As You Like It* traditionally sink or swim on the charm and fortitude of its Rosalind and the appeal and romanticism of its Orlando," she writes. "However, it's these characters' tender interactions with lesser characters like the servant Adam and a young country girl named Audrey—nicely portrayed by Jewish actors Asher Kaufman and Dani Shappiro, respectively—that give them greater dimension and definition."

Dani Shappiro, not a Jew.

"Not long ago," she continues, as if envisioning a Pulitzer in her future, "a local production transported Shakespeare's tragedy *Romeo and Juliet* to Mussolini's Italy, with the Capulets being fascists and the hated Montagues being a prominent Jewish clan forced to wear yellow Stars of David. Sincere in its intentions, that production was misguided in its execution. In his North Coast Theater directorial debut, Michael Price effectively reimagines this comedy in the American Wild West. And he addresses the Jewish question with greater sensitivity and understatement by keeping old Adam alive for the final wedding scene as if to suggest that his Jewishness has a place in the new world order."

What the fuck?!

Later in the review she writes: "And Adam, weeping openly and honestly during the marriage celebration and while being held up for emotional support by Orlando and

Rosalind during the curtain call, adds layers of poignancy to this production's powerful message of inclusiveness."

The review has already received several thousand "likes" and "loves" in the reader reaction section at the end of the online article and, much to my dismay, nearly as many shares. My email mailbox is full, and Facebook and LinkedIn alert me to record-level traffic.

That evening, as I head toward the stage door of the Hedley Theatre for our next sold-out performance, I notice that the North Coast Theater marketing team has already pulled quotes from the reviews, turned them into window cards and marquee banners, and put them on display. They read:

A SIMPLY GLORIOUS ROMP—*SCENE*

A COMIC TRIUMPH—*THE PLAIN DEALER*

NOTHING SHORT OF WONDERFUL
—*THE NEWS-HERALD*

ONE OF NORTH COAST'S MOST KOSHER COMEDIES
—*CLEVELAND JEWISH CHRONICLE*

CHAPTER 27

Moving Forward

Parting is such sweet sorrow that I shall
say goodnight till it be morrow.

Romeo and Juliet (Act II, Scene II)

*A*s the production run of *As You Like It* draws to a close, Andrew Ganz invites me to his office to give me good-natured grief about that *Cleveland Jewish Chronicle* review and to ask if I am at all interested in staying on with the company as the show moves on to Taos for a few weeks. The piles of résumés, head shots, and discarded scripts that cluttered the room when I first asked Andrew for an audition have since grown taller and threaten to make the place uninhabitable.

I'm flattered by the offer and my fear of Shakespeare has been in a functional state of suspension. The only symptoms have been some pre-show butterflies, routinely sweating through my costume halfway through the first act, and some minor post-traumatic quaking on the drive home from the theater. After the first of several double performance dates— when we stage a 3 p.m. matinee and a 8 p.m. evening show— the costumer knows to wait for me in the wings with a spray bottle of Febreze and a hand dryer between performances.

A huge roll of elastic sports tape for my thighs has myste-riously replaced the stage putty in my makeup kit.

Andrew also mentions that an ensemble player who committed to, but had not yet signed on to, the upcom-ing musical *Sweeney Todd* took work elsewhere. He asks if I would be interested in coming on board for that production as well.

"We rehearse and open in Taos and you'd already be there doing *As You Like It*. The run of *Sweeney Todd* ends back in Cleveland. You could write more behind-the-scenes pieces for your paper, and this time they would take place in one of Stephen Sondheim's most memorable musicals."

I actually give this a moment of serious contemplation.

But then the concept of singing Sondheim—with its dense, complex lyrics and enigmatic melodies meant to challenge the ear, not soothe it—settles in, and it's Mt. Everest all over again. The oxygen rapidly leaves the room and my ears start to ring as if I'm concussed. And I'm confident that there are a dozen grinning, singing, meat pie-slinging Angela Lans-burys waiting for me on the street outside Andrew Ganz's office. I lean on a nearby stalagmite of audition DVDs for support, which crumbles under my touch.

CHAPTER 28

The Road Not Taken

Well, God give them wisdom that have it. And
those that are fools, let them use their talents.

Twelfth Night (Act I, Scene V)

SO GWEN WILL be replacing me at the *Chronicle* for the
three months I'll be in Taos performing *As You Like It* and
Sweeney Todd.

Sure, while standing in Andrew Ganz's office I heard that
voice in my head yell, "Run." And, at home, I listened to
every one of Patty's logical arguments to stay home. "You
have nothing more to prove to yourself" was her most per-
suasive. Even Mark, my managing editor, noted that this
excursion into embedded journalism was a huge success but
"it was time to get back to business as usual."

I ignored them all, recalling the brave words Duke Senior
shared with his band of faithful lords after leaving the cruel
but civilized world of his brother's court for the unknown in
the Forest of Arden: "Sweet are the uses of adversity which,
like the toad, ugly and venomous, wears yet a precious jewel
in his head. And this our life, exempt from public haunt,
finds tongues in trees, books in the running brooks, sermons
in stones, and good in everything."

Bring on adversity, for addressing it head-on and without hesitation is what we little people do. I still have much to find in the words of Shakespeare and in the lyrics of Sondheim.

One thing I have found is that Jaques' famous monologue about the world being a stage means more to me than a lofty metaphor about life. The speech is delivered while Orlando is offstage fetching the dying Adam so he can have a final meal and feel the warmth of a campfire with friends before Shakespeare banishes him from the pages of his play. Although there is nothing in the text to support this, I believe that Jaques is referencing the old man when his speech identifies the seven theatrical acts that constitute a life. And after watching it delivered for twenty-five performances from the wings, I've come to believe that the speech speaks volumes about my journey playing Adam, during which my world has quite literally been a stage. Says Jaques:

> All the world's a stage,
> And all the men and women merely players;
> They have their exits and their entrances,
> And one man in his time plays many parts,
> His acts being seven ages. At first, the infant,
> Mewling and puking in the nurse's arms.
> Then the whining schoolboy, with his satchel
> And shining morning face, creeping like snail
> Unwillingly to school.

I remember quite clearly the proud moment of my highly public mewling and puking in the North Coast Theater parking lot outside of Andrew Ganz's office when I learned I was cast in this play. In a sudden state of panic, the world spun around me and I felt as vulnerable and overwhelmed as a newborn. And, yeah, that was me whining like a child while desperately attempting to learn my lines, not so much unwillingly going to school as unable and woefully ill-equipped to learn.

And then the lover,
Sighing like furnace, with a woeful ballad
Made to his mistress' eyebrow. Then a soldier,
Full of strange oaths and bearded like the pard,
Jealous in honor, sudden and quick in quarrel,
Seeking the bubble reputation
Even in the cannon's mouth. And then the justice,
In fair round belly with good capon lined,
With eyes severe and beard of formal cut,
Full of wise saws and modern instances;
And so he plays his part.

Once I managed to shed my script and stumble my way through Shakespeare-speak, I most certainly became a lover of the woeful ballads and strange oaths I was asked to recite on stage as Adam, all the while soldiering through what I thought were discouraging notes meant to undermine these efforts. My bubble reputation as a capable actor was established in the rehearsal room and in the bar across the street, where I bought adult beverages for my cast mates and shared stories of past exploits on stage that served as my wise saws and modern stances.

The sixth age shifts
Into the lean and slippered pantaloon,
With spectacles on nose and pouch on side;

His youthful hose, well saved, a world too wide
For his shrunk shank, and his big manly voice,
Turning again toward childish treble, pipes
And whistles in his sound.

With my shank most assuredly shrunk coupled with ill-fitting boots—a size too small rather than a world too wide—that was me dancing the two-step with Orlando with disastrous results that once again turned me into a mewling and immobile child.

Last scene of all,
That ends this strange eventful history,
Is second childishness and mere oblivion,
Sans teeth, sans eyes, sans taste, sans everything.

Well, this scene has not yet been played out by me, but I can see my dad, Lenny, preparing for his inevitable entrance. Though neither of us are sans anything except for the full head of hair we always took for granted, we have both come to realize that life is fleeting and needs to be embraced, without fear, for however long we are given.

And so with my little-girl whimper in check and my performance anxiety on hold, I'm ready to hit the road and further test my hamstrings and my inner demons in the beguiling worlds of *As You Like It* and *Sweeney Todd*.

My therapist friend Larry calls this the "Let the Healing Continue" Tour. I'm having t-shirts made.

Acknowledgments

*T*HIS NOVEL IS dedicated to my wife, Judy, who was instrumental in getting this book out of my head, onto the page, and into print.

And it was inspired by the late Great Lakes Theater performer Dougfred Miller, who was one of those actors who bathed in the waters of *Twelfth Night's* picturesque beachfront property and patiently taught me how to swim.

I'm terribly grateful to my dear friends and beloved family members who are avid readers and writers, communication professionals, and/or all-around smart people. Some read earlier drafts of this work and had plenty to say, much of it making its way between the covers. They are: AJ Abelman, Zach Bartz, Ryan Abelman, Chelsea Abelman, Larry Moss, Chris Page, Eric Coble, Fred Sternfeld, Randi Sternfeld, Nancy Minter, Steve Minter, Gwendolyn Kochur, Carol Pribble, and Rich Leder.

Thanks to *Cleveland Jewish News* publisher Kevin S. Adelstein, *News-Herald* editor Mark Meszoros, and *Chagrin Valley Times* editor Ellen J. Kleinerman, who granted permission to use excerpts from my published work that appear here under Asher Kaufman's byline.

The Phil Donahue Show story that appears in Chapter 6 was first told by the author in "How It Feels To Be Raw Meat," *The Plain Dealer*, February 4, 1995.

The referenced texts that offer descriptions of theater critics in the late-1700s in Chapter 8 are Irving Wardle, *Theatre Criticism* (London: Routledge, 1992), 16–17, and Michael Feingold, "Theater Criticism Reconfigured," *Village Voice*, August 11, 2009, www.villagevoice.com/2009/08/11/theater-criticism-reconfigured.

The script referenced in Chapter 10 is Juliet Dusinbee (ed.), *Arden Shakespeare: As You Like It* (London: Thomas Learning, 2006).

Michael Price's eloquent Chapter 15 description of *As You Like It* comes from director Edward Morgan and is attributed to the fictitious character with his permission.

Quotes in Chapter 19 by James S. Shapiro are from his book *Shakespeare and the Jews* (Columbia University Press, 1996), pp. 228-29, and are recast as an interview with his permission.

Magic 8 Ball is a registered trademark of Mattel, Inc.

No Fear Shakespeare is published by Spark Publishing, sparknotes.com/nofear/shakespeare.